I0762280

The BIRTH, LIFE and DEATH of

SCARAMOUCH

Harrewyn fecit
SCARAMOUCHE
entrant au Theatre.

The BIRTH, LIFE and DEATH of
SCARAMOUCH

BY

Master ANGELO CONSTANTINI

Known as MEZZETIN, *Comedian in Ordinary*, of the *Italian* Company of Players in the service of the King of *France*

Translated from the FIRST EDITION *published at* PARIS, 1695

BY

CYRIL W. BEAUMONT

Together with MEZZETIN'S *dedicatory Poems and* LORET'S *rhymed News-letters concerning* SCARAMOUCH, *now first rendered into* ENGLISH *Verse*

BY

EDMUND BLUNDEN

Embellished with four illustrations

LONDON
Published by C. W. BEAUMONT
at the *Sign* of the *Harlequin's Bat*
75, Charing Cross Road

MDCCCCXXIV

NOVERRE PRESS

First published in 1924

This facsimile reprint published in 2012 by
The Noverre Press
Southwold House
Isington Road
Binsted
Hampshire
GU34 4PH

© 2011 The Noverre Press

ISBN 978-1-906830-40-3

A CIP catalogue record for this book is available from the British Library

Printed and made in England.

This *English* Translation of Constantini's *La Vie de Scaramouche* is DEDICATED

To DE V. PAYEN-PAYNE

In memory of many hours, as pleasant as profitable, passed in his company,

By

His Friend,

THE PUBLISHER.

TRANSLATOR'S PREFACE

"THERE is no real biography of Alexandre Dumas," states Mr. Andrew Lang in his witty and learned preface to an English translation of *Les Trois Mousquetaires*. The same may be said of Tiberio Fiorilli, the celebrated actor of the Mask of Scaramouch, whose stage career of over sixty years must surely be one of the longest in the history of the theatre.

I had hoped, in preparing an English translation of Constantini's *La Vie de Scaramouche*, that whether my labours were ill or well received to have been able to claim the simple merit of being first in the field. But at the very moment of completion of my task I happened on an English edition "Translated by *A. R.* from the *French* Copy: Printed at *Paris*, 1695. *LONDON*, Printed for *Robert Gifford*, and are to be sold at his Shop in *Old-Bedlam*, without *Bishopsgate*. 1696."

This extremely rare book is, to the best of my knowledge, the only English translation. If my conjecture is correct a new translation is overdue. The edition mentioned does not conform so closely to the text of the original as my own, neither does it contain a rendering of Constantini's complimentary verses or the rhymed news-letters of Loret relating to Fiorilli. For the English versification of these I am indebted to Mr. Edmund Blunden. I desire also to record my warmest thanks to my friend Mr. de V. Payen-Payne for having carefully overlooked the proofs of the present volume. I have chosen to retain the original title of the work, since it is clear from the *Privilege* set at the end of the first edition that the author's intention was to entitle his book *The Birth, Life and Death of Scaramouch.*[1]

The author, Angelo Constantini, though not the originator of the Mask called Mezzetin (Mezzetino), was the first to dress this character in the striped red and white garments which have become characteristic of the part. Angelo was the son of Constantino Constantini, whose father was a merchant in a large way of business at Verona.

At first, Constantino devoted his attention to trade, set up a factory and made important discoveries in new methods of dyeing cloth. Then he fell in love with an actress of a travelling company and, although a married man, abandoned his business and followed the player, forcing his wife and two sons to accompany him. In turn attracted by the lodestar of the stage, he played the character of Gradelino, in which he achieved considerable success. He first acted at Paris, with the Italian Comedians, about 1687. Being very musical he was charged by his fellows to arrange the music that formed part of the performances. There is a story that he conceived the unfortunate notion of singing on the stage a song composed in Italy against the French which was so ill received that he never dared to appear in public again.

He had two sons, Gian-Battista, who played the Mask of Octave (Ottavio), and Angelo, the author of our book. He also had a natural son by his mistress called Antonio

[1] " Il est permis à ANGELO CONSTANTINI, Comédien Ordinaire de Sa Majesté, de faire imprimer un Livre intitulé *La Naissance, Vie & Mort de Scaramouche.*"

who made an unsuccessful *début* as Harlequin at Paris in 1739.

In 1682, Angelo, who had appeared with success in Italy, joined a company at Paris, in which Fiorilli as Scaramouch was the leading player, to understudy the celebrated Harlequin Domenico Biancolelli who, however, a very conscientious actor, gave him few opportunities to display his talent. Constantini, finding that the troupe had no second *zany* or Brighella, abandoned the mask associated with this early buffoon character and devising the costume already described called himself Mezzetin, which is a type of valet-adventurer. He made his *début* at Paris on October 11, 1683, in *Arlequin Protée*,[1] playing Glaucus-Mezzetin to Domenico's Protée-Arlequin.

When Domenico died in 1688, Constantini adopted the mask and parti-coloured garb of Harlequin but retained his name of Mezzetin.[2] He had very pleasing and expressive features and when he appeared in his new dress the audience shouted " No mask ! " Hence he discarded this portion of Harlequin's equipment and continued to play without it until Evaristo Gherardi joined the company, making his first Paris appearance on October 1, 1689, as Harlequin in *Le Divorce Forcé*, with such success that Constantini returned to his former part of Mezzetin. The latter continued to play until 1697 when the theatre, the Hôtel de Bourgogne, was closed as a result of the performance of *La Fausse Prude* in which Constantini was guilty of lese-majesty by making satirical allusions to Madame de Maintenon. He then went to Germany and joined a company at

[1] A comedy in three acts by Monsieur D***. It is given in Gherardi's *Théâtre Italien*.

[2] See Plate II., facing p. xii.

Brunswick when August I., King of Poland and Elector of Saxony, offered him an engagement to form a company to play Italian comedy and sing Italian opera. He returned to France in 1698 on a recruiting expedition and performed his task so well that the Elector made him his Treasurer of Entertainments and even ennobled him.

His sense of proportion unbalanced by his unexpected good fortune and the favours heaped upon him, he had the audacity to become enamoured of the king's mistress, declared his passion and the better to further his ambition endeavoured to exalt himself at the expense of his benefactor. This insolence caused him to be imprisoned in the Castle of Königstein where he remained for twenty years until, as the result of the entreaties of a later favourite of the Elector's, he was set free.

He departed to Verona and travelled to Paris, eager to renew acquaintance with the scenes of his former triumphs. There he joined the Regent's company of Italian Comedians and reappeared on February 5, 1729, in a revival of *La Foire Saint-Germain*.[1] He made a considerable success and pleased greatly by his appeal to the public's goodwill, to whom he addressed the following verse :—

Mezzetin, par d'heureux talents,
  Voudrait vous satisfaire.
Quoiqu'il soit depuis très-longtemps
  Presque sexagénaire,
Il rajeunira de trente ans
S'il peut encore vous plaire.

He gave in all some five performances, the clamour

[1] A celebrated comedy by Messieurs Regnard et du F***, first represented at the Hôtel de Bourgogne, December 16, 1695. It is included in Gherardi's *Théâtre Italien*.

The illustration designed to celebrate the re-opening, on September 1, 1688, of the theatre of the Palais Royal. It had been closed for a month by the Italian Comedians as a sign of mourning for the loss of their beloved comrade, the great *Harlequin*, Domenico Biancolelli, who died on August 2. Angelo Constantini, who played the Mask of *Mezzetin*, being chosen to succeed Domenico as *Harlequin*, is seen receiving from Columbine the mask and bat, the attributes of his new part. In the background can be observed Domenico's tomb, with his widow in tears before it. Tiberio Fiorilli, in his character of *Scaramouch*, is the third figure from the right. (Reproduced from the *Grand Almanach Historique* for 1689, published by Pierre Landry.)

for places being so great that the usual price of admission was doubled. Three months later he left Paris and returned to Verona, where he died at the end of the year.

At this point the reader may well enquire as to the reception of his *Vie de Scaramouche.* If the number of editions is any indication it would appear to have met with unusual favour. The first edition was published at Paris by Claude Barbin in 1695. A second edition was issued in the same year and a third published at Lyons by Thomas Amaulry. The book was reprinted at Brussels in 1699 and 1708, also at Troyes in 1729. It is included in Blismon's *Trésor des Arlequinades* (1856) and was reprinted in a limited edition by Bonnassies in 1876, with an excellent introduction by Louis Moland. I have mentioned the English edition of 1696. It was also published in Italian at Venice in 1726, under the title *Nascita, Vita, e Morte del famoso Scaramuzza Comico Napolitano.* I have cited only the various issues known to me; it is quite possible that there are others.

In view of the undoubted warmth of its reception it is curious, in references to Constantini, to find his book described so frequently as a tissue of lies. This opinion is, I suspect, very largely based on Gherardi's remarks in the *Avertissement* to his *Théâtre Italien, ou Recueil Général de toutes les Comédies & Scènes Françoises jouées par les Comediens Italiens du Roi pendant tout le temps qu'ils ont été au Service*, first published in 1700. There he speaks of pirated editions of his work which, " worth less than nothing, have been composed, so it is said, by the author of *Arlequiniana*,[1] or by the author

[1] By Carlo Cotolendi, first published at Paris, 1694.

of *La Vie de Scaramouche*. It is true that these two authors are so alike in the poverty of their style and in the falsity of the events which they relate, that it is easy to be deceived and mistake one for the other without much difficulty. These two writers are equally bad, and both historians equally untrue, each of them attributing to his hero things which he neither did nor thought of. I excuse however the author of *La Vie de Scaramouche* for making his book so detestable since he has been obliged to do this to conform to the ability of the person who wishes to put his name to it."

What is the explanation of this virulent attack? The reason is not far to seek. As M. Moland reminds us,[1] if the Hôtel de Bourgogne were closed and the company suppressed as a result of the performance of *La Fausse Prude* in which Constantini made indiscreet allusions to the king's mistress, it can well be imagined that Gherardi, one of the principal actors and moreover director of the company, would not lightly forgive the author of this double blow to his pocket and his ambition. Gherardi made strenuous efforts, through his friends at court, to obtain a reversal of the king's decision to close his theatre, but without success. This could only have increased his sense of annoyance.

It is true that Mezzetin's book is not remarkable for its literary style. It is true that many of the incidents described have more than a savour of scenes borrowed from the Italian Comedy. Doubtless Constantini wrote his life of Scaramouch to meet an anticipated popular demand and hence feared to make the book too serious; but his work, though often inaccurate and deficient, is by no means a pure fabrication. The various farcical embellishments with which Mezzetin and his

[1] Preface to *La Vie de Scaramouche,* reprint of 1876, p. xxx.

collaborator (if he had one) chose to season their *Life of Scaramouch* are probably an endeavour to eke out a paucity of biographical material. It will be remarked that Mezzetin, in his preface, himself comments on the smallness of his book. And seeing that the subject of the history was a celebrated actor, that the author was a player also, that at the time of publication the Italian Comedy was so greatly in the public favour; what could be more natural than that Mezzetin should introduce scenes which when played on the stage had amused so highly?

On the other hand, one is inclined to believe that some of the fantastic incidents described are not wholly without foundation. Listen to this anecdote regarding Mezzetin recorded by the brothers Parfaict.[1] Constantini had dedicated a play to the Duc de Saint-Agnan, who was wont to reward liberally such courtesies. Accordingly he presented himself at the Duke's house. "The porter, suspecting the object of his visit, refused him entrance. He overcame his scruples by promising him a third of the recompense he would receive. On the stairs he met the head footman who had also to be bribed by the promise of another third. Having at last arrived at the ducal apartments he encountered the duke's valet, whose opposition was only removed by the promise of the last third. Mezzetin, on seeing the duke, cried: 'My lord, here is a theatrical piece which I take the liberty of presenting to you, and for which I beg that you will reward me by ordering me to be given a hundred lashes.' The duke, amazed at this request, enquired the reason of it. 'It is, my lord,' said Mezzetin, 'that to contrive to reach your presence I have been compelled to promise

[1] *Histoire de l'ancien Théâtre Italien.* Paris. 1767.

to your porter, to your lackey and to your valet each one third of whatever you may have the goodness to give me.' The duke severely reprimanded his servants and sent a hundred louis to the wife of Mezzetin who had entered into no promises."

It is time to consider the career of Scaramouch. Tiberio Fiorilli was born at Naples on November 9, 1608. The day and month are stated by Lelong,[1] who bases his conclusion on a portrait of the actor drawn by Henri de Gissey, *dessinateur ordinaire des Ballets du Roi*. Mezzetin tells us that his father was a Captain of Horse and that he had an elder brother called Trappolino. But very little is known of his life prior to his coming to Paris. It is certain that he married at Naples an Italian named Lorenzo-Elisabeta del Campo. Sand [2] gives an account of the event that led to this first marriage. It would appear that Fiorilli, despite his being the son of a Captain, was at the age of twenty-five employed as a servant by the leading lady of a company of actors which then enjoyed a considerable reputation at Naples. In addition he acted as general utility man and filled small parts as occasion demanded. One day his employer's laundress told him that her daughter's greatest friend was to be married and that her daughter was to be one of the bridesmaids; knowing him to be a fellow of lively humour, she invited him to the wedding, which was celebrated with an abundance of eating and drinking. Fiorilli, as Mezzetin informs us, was an excellent table companion. In the course of a dance, the wine having mounted to his head, in an access of passion he seized

[1] *Bibliothèque Historique de la France*, quoted Jal (A.) *Dictionnaire Critique de Biographie et d'Histoire*. Paris. 1867.

[2] Sand (Maurice), *Masques et Bouffons*. 2 Vols. 1860. Vol. 2, p. 261.

upon and kissed the bridesmaid. This insult having been offered in public was regarded in the most serious light and reparable only by marriage. The next day the laundress and her family called on Fiorilli's employer and demanded justice.

The culprit, so far from defending himself, could not even recall the offence of which he was accused. Finally, as a result of his employer's representations, he married the girl. It will be remarked that this story does not agree with the romantic courtship related by Mezzetin. Some time after their marriage they joined a troupe of comedians. Fiorilli assumed the name of Scaramouch, while his wife played the part of a Soubrette, calling herself Marinette.

Mezzetin states that Fiorilli was the creator of the character known as Scaramouch. This is incorrect. In Callot's *Balli di Sfessania* (? 1622) there is a representation of a *Scaramuccia* of the Fedeli company. This personage is depicted in a posture of defence; a rapier in his right hand, and his left, wrapped round with a cloak, raised on guard. Except that he wears a mask and his cap is decorated with two long feathers, there is no vital difference in his costume from that worn by Fiorilli. Scaramouch is derived from the Italian *scaramuzzia*, meaning a little fighter or skirmisher, and this Mask is a descendant of the ancient figure of comedy known as the Captain, who is a braggart, a boaster and a liar. He breathes hell-fire and slaughter. But if his victim's eyebrow but frowns or his hand strays to his sword-hilt, then the Captain's courage evaporates like the gas from a pricked toy balloon. He concocts so many legends of his prowess that by sheer force of repetition he ends by believing them himself. In war, he outrivals the exploits of

Bayard; in love, his amorous propensities would put to shame those of Casanova.

The Captain is one of the most popular types in the world's literature. He is to be recognised as Pyrogopolinices in Plautus' *The Braggart Captain*, in Shakespeare's Falstaff and Pistol, as Captain Bluffe in Congreve's *The Old Bachelor*, as Capitaine Fracasse in Gautier's romance of the same name; Scarron wrote a one-act piece on this character entitled *Les Boutades du Capitan Matamore* (1646)—but the list grows interminable. In Italy, "the Captain, says M. Frederic Mercey,[1] antedates the Spanish dominion; we consider him the contemporary of all those formidable leaders of Italian bands who distinguished themselves in those famous encounters in which a horse, by turning its head or its tail, might suffice to bring about the loss or gain of a battle."

Sand [2] says the first Captains date from the fifteenth century. They wore a buff jacket, a long sword, a steel morion and a flesh-coloured mask with terrific moustaches. Then when Italy came under the rule of Charles V., the Captain became Spanish in style and was known as Captain Matamoros. "Towards 1680," as Riccoboni [3] states, "the Spanish Captains came to an end in Italy, and the old Italian Captain having been forgotten, it became necessary to find in the companies of Neapolitan comedians an actor to replace the Spanish Captain; thus Scaramuccia was created. In Italy this personage has never had any other character than that of the Captain." But in France the character of Scaramouch must have been revived sooner, since,

[1] Quoted Sand, *Masques et Bouffons*. Vol. 1, p. 184.
[2] *Op. cit.*
[3] Riccoboni (Luigi), *Histoire du Théâtre Italien*. 2 Vols. Paris. 1728-31.

The Mask of *Scaramouch*, circa 1645, from an engraving in Sand's *Masques et Bouffons* (1860).

Plate III

as we shall see later, Fiorilli played this part in Paris certainly in 1644, probably earlier still.

Scaramouch is always dressed in black. Riccoboni [1] says that " in cut it is an imitation of the Spanish dress, which, in the city of Naples, had long been the dress of courtiers, of magistrates and of soldiers." According to Sand,[2] Scaramouch's breeches were at first wide and afterwards he assumed those which have remained traditional to the character. The girdle has sometimes been of cloth like the costume, sometimes of leather. Fiorilli abandoned the mask of the early figure of comedy and played with floured face and blackened eyebrows and moustache. Scaramouch has all the qualities of the Captain and something of the Harlequin, for he can be agile, witty, gay and an adept at getting out of scrapes. He is nearly always the servant of a decayed gentleman or petty bourgeois.

I have mentioned some slight particulars of Fiorilli's parentage, but he had also a make-believe ancestry. In Act I., Scene VII. of *Colombine Avocat Pour et Contre*,[3] the following dialogue takes place :—

CINTHIO (approaching Scaramouch). *Come vi chiamate ?* (What is your name ?)

SCARAMOUCH. What is my name ?

CINTHIO. *Si, il vostro nome, qual è ?* (Yes, what is your name ?)

SCARAMOUCH. *Il mio nome, signor, è* (My name, sir, is) Scaramuzza, Memeo Squaquara, Tammera, Catambera, *e figlio di* (a son of) Cocumaro and of Madonna Papara Trent'ova, e Iunze, e Dunze, e Tiracarunze, *per servire à vossignoria* (to serve your lordship).

[1] Riccoboni (Luigi), *Histoire du Théâtre Italien.* 2 Vols. Paris. 1728–31.

[2] *Op. cit.*

[3] A comedy in three acts by Monsieur D***. Included in Gherardi's *Théâtre Italien.*

Little is known of Fiorilli's life prior to his coming to Paris. Mezzetin's assertion that he achieved the greatest success and was the favourite of princes is borne out by Gherardi, who states that " a great prince who saw him play at Rome, remarked: '*Scaramuccia non parla, e dise gran cose.*'[1] And on the comedy being finished he made him a present of a coach and six horses. He was always the delight of all the princes who knew him and our invincible monarch[2] never wearied of heaping favours upon him."

Fiorilli first came to Paris between 1639 and 1640, during the last years of Louis XIII., if we may credit the anecdote related by the brothers Parfaict.[3] One day Scaramouch being in the Dauphin's room, with the Queen present, this prince manifested the greatest ill humour, so that nothing could calm his tears and cries. Scaramouch begged the Queen to permit him to take the prince in his arms, since he thought he could appease him. The Queen assented and the comedian, by the means of his wonderful mimic powers, not only stopped his cries but made him wish to laugh; which so excited the prince that, giving way to a natural inclination, he soiled the hands and clothes of Scaramouch, to the great amusement of the company.

At this time the different companies of comedians invited to Paris did not take up their abode there, for they were not yet an established institution. They were sent for and the expenses of their journey paid, and after a season they returned home.

When Richelieu died in 1642 he was succeeded by Cardinal Mazarin, a great lover of theatrical enter-

[1] "Scaramouch, without speaking, says a great deal."
[2] Louis XIV.
[3] *Op. cit.*

tainments, who invited to Paris a company of the best Italian comedians, including Fiorilli. It is quite certain that Fiorilli was in Paris during 1644 for M. Jal[1] has found in the Parish Records of Saint-Germain-l'Auxerrois the following entry: "Du jeudy unziesme d'aoust 1644, fut baptisé Louis, fils de Tiberio Fiorilly (*sic*), comédien de la Royne, et d'Isabelle del Campo, sa femme; le parrain, maistre Claude Auvry, prestre, abbé, tenant pour monseigneur l'éminentissime cardinal Mazarin; la marraine, dame Marie Indret, femme d'honneur de la Royne, tenante pour Anne d'Autriche, Royne mère, régente de France." When Cardinal Mazarin stood godfather to Fiorilli's son Louis, it is not unlikely that, as Mezzetin says, Cardinal Chigi performed the same office for an elder son. This was not an unusual proceeding; in 1611, Marie de Medici had stood godmother for a child of Tristano Martinelli, the Harlequin of the Gelosi company. Fiorilli's son Louis died at the age of two and a half, being buried on December 14, 1646.

Fiorilli was a member of the troupe that played at the Petit-Bourbon Theatre in 1645. It was composed of Pantaloon, Harlequin, Mezzetin, Trivelino, Isabelle, Columbine, the Doctor, Scaramouch, Aurelia and the singers Gabriella Locatelli, Giulia Gabrielli and Marguerite Bartolozzi. The machinist to the troupe was the celebrated Giacomo Torelli da Fano. These players presented on November 14, 1645, *La Finta Pazza* (*La Folle Supposée*) by the famous Italian poet Giulio Strozzi. The company left Paris towards the end of 1647 owing to the troubles of the Fronde.

In 1653, a new troupe arrived which included

[1] Jal (A.), *Dictionnaire Critique de Biographie et d'Histoire.* Paris. 1867.

several players well known to Paris audiences, such as Tiberio Fiorilli (Scaramouch), Locatelli (Trivelino) and Brigida Bianchi (Aurelia). They played at the Petit-Bourbon Theatre and according to Sand [1] this company was the first definitely to settle in Paris. Loret celebrates the event thus :—

THE HISTORIC MUSE OF LORET FOR
THE 10TH AUGUST, 1653.

Une troupe de gens comiques,
Venus des climats italiques,
Dimanche dernier, tout de bon,
Firent dans le Petit-Bourbon,
L'ouverture de leur théâtre
Par un sujet assez folâtre.
Où l'archiplaisant Trivelin,
Qui n'a pas le nez aquilin,
Fit et dit tout plein de folies
Qui semblèrent assez jolies.
Au rapport de certains témoins,
Scaramouche n'en fit pas moins
Mais pour enchanter les oreilles,
Pâmer, pleurer, faire merveilles,
Mademoiselle Béatrix
Emporta ce jour-là le prix.

The performances were given between two and five o'clock in the afternoon, the badly lighted streets of Paris being considered dangerous after dark owing to their being infested by footpads. In October, 1658, this company shared the theatre with Molière's troupe of French comedians. The Italians played on the *jours extraordinaires*, that is, Mondays, Wednesdays, Thursdays and Saturdays. In May, 1659, some members of the company, including Fiorilli, took part in an entertainment given by Cardinal Mazarin to the Court at Vincennes.

[1] *Op. cit.*

In July, the Italians departed to their native country, and in October there arose the rumour that Fiorilli had been drowned in the Rhône, which inspired Loret, in his news-letter for the eleventh of that month, to write the funeral ode of Scaramouch. The news being proved false, Loret wrote a poem of rejoicing. The players returned to Paris in 1661. They appear to have given a month's season of performances at Fontainebleau before re-opening during January at the Palais-Royal Theatre, which as before they shared with Molière and his company. Fiorilli was the Scaramouch; the Harlequin was Domenico Biancolelli, one of the most celebrated actors of this character. This is the Domenico cited in Mezzetin's preface.

Molière lived on excellent terms with the Italians. He seems never to have missed an opportunity of attending their performances to learn all that he could of their art. He was a great admirer of Fiorilli, and is said to have received from him lessons in the art of mime. Below an engraving of Scaramouch by Bonnart there is the following verse :—

Cet illustre Comédien
Atteignit de son art l'agréable manière
Il fut le Maître de Molière
Et la nature fut le sien.

The Italian Comedians received, as Mezzetin states, an annual salary of 15,000 livres. In addition each member received a bonus when playing before the Court. Further, favourite players of the king received substantial presents from him. Fiorilli seems to have had many such gifts. M. Jal[1] quotes from the *Etats du Trésor* for 1662 a gift of 300 livres to "Tiberio

[1] *Op. cit.*

Scaramouche," another of 430 livres " in consideration of his services," and a further sum of 600 livres for his travelling expenses to and from Italy.

In 1664 he received another gift of 400 livres : " to go from Paris to Florence according to His Majesty's commands." It is probable that on this occasion " Marinette " stayed behind in Italy.

Two years later he married his son Silvio Bernardo to Marie de Roussel de Lamy.

To celebrate the occasion, the father caused a deed of settlement[1] to be drawn up, by which he made over all his estate to this son, retaining, however, the use of it during his lifetime and stipulating that a certain portion should fall to the share of his other surviving son Charles Louis, a canon of Troyes Cathedral.

In 1668 Fiorilli returned to Italy, the king giving him the sum of 600 livres for the purpose. The actor was then sixty years old. He went to Florence to see his wife, but it would appear that they lived in ill harmony since, in 1670, he requested and obtained the king's permission to return to Paris, where he arrived in August or September. So great was the public's desire to see him that the other theatres were almost deserted, Molière even being hard pressed to find money with which to pay his company. It was only when he produced his *Bourgeois Gentilhomme* on November 23, 1670, that his theatre began to fill again.

Fiorilli, ree from the ill humours of his wife and having his sons well provided for, began to turn his thoughts to a life of pleasure. He had a *liaison* with a certain Anne Doffan by whom he had a son. M. Jal[2]

[1] This document is quoted in full in Campardon (E.), *Les Comédiens du Roi de la Troupe Italienne.* 1880. Vol. I., p. 226.
[2] *Op. cit.*

The Mask of *Scaramouch* from an engraving in Riccoboni's *Histoire de l'ancien Théâtre Italien* (1728–31).

Plate IV

gives the certificate of baptism in the Parish Records of Saint-Germain-l'Auxerrois : " Du mercredi 8 novembre 1673, fut baptisé Tibère-François, fils de Tibère Fiorily (*sic*), Napolitain, officier du roi, et de damoiselle Anne Doffan, sa femme, rue de l'Arbre-Sec."

It is possible that this Anne Doffan may be the baker's daughter of the episode described by Mezzetin. She is described as "*femme*," a false statement, since Marinette was still living.

Did Fiorilli ever play Scaramouch in London? This question has often been raised as the result of a note by Evelyn in his Diary for September 29, 1675, wherein he records : " I saw the Italian Scaramuccio act before the King at Whitehall, people giving money to come in, which was very scandalous and never so before at Court-diversions. Having seen him act before in Italy many years past, I was not averse from seeing the most excellent of that kind of folly." The familiar use of the word Scaramuccio, the fact that people were willing to pay for a sight of him (which Evelyn says was " never so before at Court-diversions "), the statement that the diarist had seen him act in Italy " many years past," and that he praises the actor's performance as being " the most excellent of that kind of folly," suggest very strongly that the unnamed player of Scaramouch was Tiberio Fiorilli.

This supposition is further strengthened by numerous references to Scaramouch in contemporary English dramatic literature. Dryden, in his Epilogue to the University of Oxford spoken by Mr. Hart at the acting of *The Silent Woman* (? 1673), says :—

Heaven, for our sins, this summer has thought fit
To visit us with all the plagues of wit,

A French troop first swept all things in its way;
But those hot Monsieurs were too quick to stay:
Yet, to our cost, in that short time, we find
They left their itch of novelty behind.
The Italian merry-andrews took their place,
And quite debauched the stage with lewd grimace:
Instead of wit, and humours, your delight
Was there to see two hobby-horses fight;
Stout Scaramoucha with rush lance rode in,
And ran a tilt at centaur Arlequin.
For love you heard how amorous asses brayed,[1]
And cats in gutters gave their serenade.[2]
Nature was out of countenance, and each day
Some new-born monster shown you for a play.

Ravenscroft, in the Prologue to his *Scaramouch a Philosopher, Harlequin a School-Boy, Bravo, Merchant and Magician*, A Comedy after the Italian manner, Acted at the Theatre Royal, 1677, has :—

The Poet does a dang'rous trial make,
And all the common roads of Plays forsake.
Upon the Actors it depends too much,
And who can hope ever to see two such
As the Fam'd Harlequin & Scaramouch.

Otway, in his *Friendship in Fashion*, A Comedy, As it is Acted at his Royal Highness the Duke's Theatre, London, 1678, has the following dialogue :—

Truman. And this you say is your way of wit?

Malagene. Ay, altogether this and Mimickry! I am a very good Mimick; I can act Punchinello, Scaramuchio, Harlequin, Prince Prettyman, or any thing.

It is obvious from the above examples, a tithe of the number that could be cited, that an exceptional actor

[1] *Cf.* p. 15.
[2] *Cf.* p. 16.

only could have inspired these references to his art; and Fiorilli had so associated himself with the character of Scaramouch as to be known far and wide[1] by this name.

From the other point of view, it seems strange that Constantini, who speaks of so many towns in connection with Fiorilli, does not mention that he played in London. Especially as one would think that Fiorilli would be certain to tell his biographer that he had appeared before the king of England, Charles II. That companies of Italian comedians did come to London during the Restoration is proved by an examination of the *Calendar of State Papers, Domestic Series* and *Calendar of Treasury Books* for that period which contain the following references:—

1. *Calendar of Treasury Books, April* (? 21), 1673.

   Treasurer Clifford to the Customs Commissioners to obey an order of the King that all such clothes, vestments, scenes, ornaments, necessaries and materials directly designed for the proper use of a company of Italian comedians lately arrived here should be admitted to entry as neither contraband nor prohibited and should be free of Customs.

2. *Calendar of State Papers, Domestic Series, September* 10, 1673.

   Pass for the whole band of Italian players to

[1] Olearius, when travelling in distant Persia, is reminded of Scaramouch by the strange conduct of the mourners at a funeral procession he witnesses there: "Then follow'd two bands of Musicians, who with all their might sang the *la illa illaha*, and the *Alla Ekber*, accompanying their cries with such distorted Countenances and Postures, as Scaramuzza himself would be troubled to imitate." [*Olearius (Adam), The Voyages & Travels of the Ambassadors sent by Frederick Duke of Holstein, to the Great Duke of Muscovy, and the King of Persia, etc. Trans. by John Davies, of Kidwelly, London,* 1662. *Book VI., p.* 380.]

embark themselves, their trunks &c. at any English port for any French port.

3. *Calendar of Treasury Books, September* 11, 1673.

Money warrant for 52*l.* to Phillip Packer, to be disbursed in satisfaction for the building of the Italians' stage, as agreed to be paid by His Majesty's order.

4. *Calendar of Treasury Books, September* 12, 1673.

Warrant from Treasurer Latimer to the Customs Commissioners to suffer the Italian Comedians to export in the " Merlin " yacht their proper and peculiar clothes, vestments, scenes and other necessaries, Customs free.

5. *Calendar of State Papers, Domestic Series, April* 1675.

[The Duke of Monmouth to Sir W. Lockhart.]

The King has commanded me to write to you to press the Italian players to hasten their journey, and for their better undertaking it Sir Stephen Fox will remit you by this post 200*l.* and a yacht shall be ready at their time in any convenient port they desire to embark at. On their arrival here a place will be assigned them.

6. *Calendar of Treasury Books, June* 20, 1675.

Warrant from Treasurer Danby to the Customs Commissioners to deliver to Monsieur Brunetts, Custom free, and without opening, several vestments, habits, scenes and other necessaries belonging to the Italian comedians and lately brought from France in the " Portsmouth " and " Ann " yachts.

7. *Calendar of Treasury Books, October* 22, 1675.

52*l.* paid by the Earl of St. Albans for building the stage for the Italian comedians.

8. *Calendar of Treasury Books, October* 4, 1675.

Warrant from Treasurer Danby to the Customs Commissioners to suffer the Italian comedians to export in one of the King's yachts their proper and peculiar cloths, vestments, scenes and other necessaries, Customs free.

9. *Calendar of Treasury Books, November* 11, 1678.

Warrant from Treasurer Danby to the Customs Commissioners to permit the landing, and to deliver, Customs free, the goods (6 portmanteaus, 2 great baskets and 22 trunks) belonging to the Company of the Italian comedians lately arrived and not forbidden by the late prohibitions in the Poll Act, 'the same being, as I am informed, cloaths and other necessarys for their own use.'

10. *Calendar of Treasury Books, February* 12, 1679.

Warrant from Treasurer Danby to the Customs Commissioners to permit the export to France, Customs free, on the "Merlin" (or some other) yacht of the goods of the Italian players.

11. *Calendar of State Papers, Domestic Series, February* 13, 1679.

Pass for the Band of Italian Players, now departing out of this realm with annexed list of them sent by Lord Arlington.

Examining these references, No. 1 proves that a band of Italian players arrived in London early in 1673 and, according to Nos. 2 and 4, returned to France during September of the same year. It may be that Fiorilli was a member of this troupe but I can find no details of the names of the actors. No. 5 shows that the king was eager for a further visit of this, or another, company. And it is clear from No. 6 that a troupe arrived in May or June, 1675. This is the company one of whose performances is described by Evelyn on September 29, and there is every reason to believe that Fiorilli was a member of it. In No. 3 there is a reference to an expenditure of 52*l.* " in satisfaction for the building of the Italians' stage." If it was customary to discharge all expenses attendant on the visits of the Italian companies immediately prior to, or just after, their departure, it would appear that the troupe seen by Evelyn left for France late in 1675 since there is a note (No. 7) of a similar sum having been paid in respect of a stage constructed for their use. No. 8 is further evidence of their preparations for departure. No. 9 shows that the Italians again visited London in the last quarter of 1678 and left for France, according to Nos. 10 and 11, during February of the following year.

I have examined at the Public Record Office the list of players mentioned in No. 11. This document contains thirty-five names written in a crabbed hand and, so far as I can decipher them, there is no mention of Fiorilli. Further, the list contains only three well-known names. These are Giovanni Battista Lolli who played the Doctor, Giuseppe Tortoriti who played Pasquariello, and Constantino Constantini who played Gradelino. The first acted at Paris in 1653 but the second and third did not play there until 1685 and 1687 respectively. Hence it would appear that the troupe was an inferior one. Now since the company of Italian comedians in the service of Louis XIV. was composed of the best talent available, and since it is extremely unlikely that Fiorilli, then at the height of his reputation, would have acted with any but first class players, it is very doubtful that he was a member of this company. To sum up, while there are many indications that incline one to believe that Fiorilli did come to London between the years 1673 and 1675 it cannot be so stated with certainty on the data I have so far collected.

Returning to Fiorilli's life in Paris we find that about 1680, Fiorilli became enamoured of another lady, one of doubtful reputation, aged some twenty years, whom he made his mistress and took into his house. This girl was called Marie-Robert Duval and despite the age of her lover presented him with a daughter. Here is the certificate of baptism transcribed by M. Jal [1] from the Parish Records of Saint-Eustache: " le 29 Juillet 1681, fut baptisée Anne-Elizabeth, née de ce jour de Tiberio Fiorillo (*sic*), officier du roi, gentilhomme napolitain, et de damoiselle Marie Duval, sa femme, demeurant rue de la Friperie."

Again the false declaration that the mother is his wife. Mezzetin declares that Marie Duval forsook Scaramouch to go to England with a young admirer who, however, soon abandoned her, when she returned to Paris to be forgiven and taken back by her old lover.

Marinette, who had continued to reside in Italy, died there in 1687. Scaramouch had several children as a result of this union, certainly three sons, probably five, of whom it would appear that one only, Silvio, survived him. The news of Marinette's death being brought to the king's notice by his cousin-german the Grand Duchess of Tuscany, Louis XIV., turned pious through the influence of Madame de Maintenon, exhorted him to marry Marie Duval: " en vue de rétablir l'état de sa fille et pour vivre en bon chrétien." [2] The marriage

[1] *Op. cit.*

[2] Quoted Campardon (E.), *Les Comédiens du Roi de la Troupe Italienne.*

took place on May 8, 1688, at the church of Saint-Sauveur.

The new wife, pardoned for her fault, bound in holy wedlock and proud of bearing the honoured name of famed Scaramouch will surely exert all her powers to make the old actor's last years happy. But on the contrary, poor Scaramouch lives a most miserable existence. His son Silvio, who generally resides at Florence, comes to Paris in May, 1690 ; stays with his father and again proves himself to be an arrant rogue. Five years earlier, by means of a false key, he has contrived to open his father's strong-box and rob him of a considerable sum of money. This time, he soon quarrels with the old man in endeavour to extort money from him. His efforts proving abortive, he bides his time and on the night of the fifteenth of November again succeeds in rifling the treasure chest to the extent of 7000 livres in gold and 3000 livres in precious stones.

The wife, tired of her elderly spouse, seeks consolation elsewhere ; at first clandestinely, later in so brazen a manner that she sets all the neighbours' tongues wagging. But a life of pleasure soon palls without money and her funds are low. She cajoles her husband to give her money, but the old man, despite his being half blind and half deaf, has both seen and heard too much. She rages, storms, threatens—but to no purpose. In her anger she beats him with any weapon that lies to hand, so that Scaramouch, in danger of his life, is forced to seek redress before the Commissary of the district of Saint-Eustache and Saint-Sauveur.

There is a long series of these signs of marital infelicity. In one of May 2, 1672, Fiorilli accuses his wife of having stolen from him at various times sums amounting to 8000 livres and of having sold his silver plate.[1] In another of August 11 of the same year, he accuses her of adulterous relations with a certain Lafaye. Four days later he again appears before the Commissary. It seems that the authorities had decided to send the wife for a course of correction to the convent of Sainte-Geneviève de Chaillot.

There are scenes of redoubled violence, of murderous assaults. One day, Scaramouch receives so violent a blow that he falls to the ground, unconscious.

On coming to his senses he goes to the Commissary, shows his injuries and informs him that his wife has taken his keys and is rifling his strong box. The officer goes immediately to his house and discovers the wife endeavouring to effect a removal of the furniture. On being questioned, she tells the Commissary that before going to the convent she intends to take with her the property that belongs to her.

The following day, Secretary of State de la Reynie orders Desgrez, Lieutenant of the Watch, to arrest Marie-Robert Duval, wife of Tiberio Fiorilli, and conduct her to the Refuge, a prison for women of ill fame. She remains there for a fortnight, when Desgrez is ordered to remove Marie-Robert Duval to the convent at Chaillot. Fiorilli must pay for her keep, which he refuses to do, and on September 29 the Abbess of Chaillot sets free Marie Duval, who immediately commences legal proceedings against her husband. The witnesses are called and the trial drags on a whole month. On October 29 the verdict is pronounced. Marie Duval is condemned to return to the convent of Chaillot, and Fiorilli must pay for her support. The

[1] Campardon (E.) and Longnon (A.), *La Vieillesse de Scaramouche,* quoted Moland, *op. cit.*

sentence is carried out and the next day Marie Duval is taken to the convent, where she dies during November.

On March 19, 1694, Scaramouch takes steps to ensure the legal position of Anne Elizabeth, his daughter by Marie Duval. According to Constantini, Fiorilli still played in comedy until within five years of his death, that would be about a year after his second marriage, for the great actor died on December 7, 1694, according to the certificate of burial found by M. Jal[1]: " Dudit jour, mercredi huitiesme décembre 1694, deffunct honorable homme Tiberio Fiorilly (*sic*), officier du roy, ci-devant en sa troupe de comédiens italiens, demeurant rue Tictone, décédé du septiesme du présent mois, a esté inhumé dans notre église. Signé : Silvio Fiorilli, Marc-Antoine Romagnesy [2] (*sic*)."

It may be enquired, " What became of Fiorilli's wealth ? " Mezzetin tells us that " he bequeathed to his son, who is a learned priest of considerable merit, all the estate he possessed in France and Italy, which amounted to nearly one hundred thousand crowns." This son, Charles Louis, was not present at his father's funeral. Was he dead, or was it impossible for him to leave Troyes to come to Paris ? It seems difficult to believe that Scaramouch left his money to Silvio, who had so often quarrelled with and robbed him. Nevertheless, how could he have rescinded the assignment made on the occasion of this son's marriage ? It may be that the witness to the burial certificate was another Silvio, perhaps a natural son. In any case the name of the actual beneficiary cannot be stated with certainty. At least, his daughter Anne Elizabeth cannot have been

[1] *Op. cit.*

[2] Marco Antonio Romagnesi (1633–1706). One of Fiorilli's fellow actors who played the Mask of Cinthio.

disinherited, since her father took such pains to establish her position; and we know that she was alive, since she married in 1695, at the church of Saint-Eustache, a master painter called Jean de Clermont.

And so we take leave of Scaramouch, one of the greatest actors and most popular figures of his day. The literature of the period contains frequent references to the charm of his art. He is mentioned in the letters of the Marquise de Sévigné, in the works of Molière and Racine, in the writings of Furetière and of Palaprat. Ménage[1] says of his acting: "C'était la plus parfaite pantomime que nous avons vu de nos jours." But perhaps his best epitaph, which gives an insight into his method, is to be found in the tribute paid to his memory by Gherardi in Act II. of the comedy entitled *Columbine Avocat Pour et Contre* :—

SCENE VII

The scene represents Harlequin's room

SCARAMOUCH PASQUARIELLO

Scaramouch appears and after having mended everything that is in the room, takes his guitar, seats himself in an armchair and plays whilst awaiting his master's arrival. Pasquariello comes softly behind him and beats the time of the music on his shoulders, which frightens Scaramouch terribly.

In short, it is here where that incomparable Scaramouch, who was the ornament of the Theatre and the pattern of the most illustrious Players of his age, who learned from him their art at once so difficult and so necessary to persons of their *character*, how to stir up

[1] *Ménagiana*, 1673, p. 176.

passions and depict them in the features ; it is here, I say, that for a long quarter of an hour he would make his audience die of laughter during a scene of terror in which he did not utter a single word. It must also be acknowledged that this excellent actor possessed this marvellous ability in so high a degree that he could move the hearts of his audience by the simplicity and naturalness of his mime far more than they are ordinarily moved by the charms of the most persuasive Rhetoric.[1]

CYRIL W. BEAUMONT.

[1] *L'Avocat Pour et Contre* in Gherardi's *Théâtre Italien.* Vol. I. p. 294 (Edition published 1717).

LIST OF WORKS CONSULTED

BASCHET (ARMAND) *Les Comédiens italiens à la cour de France sous Charles IX., Henri III., Henry IV., et Louis XIII.* Paris, 1882.

CAMPARDON (EMILE) *Les Comédiens du Roi de la Troupe Italienne pendant les deux derniers siècles.* Paris, 2 Vols., 1880.

CONSTANTINI (ANGELO) *La Vie de Scaramouche. Réimpression de l'édition originale* (1695). *Avec une introduction et des notes par Louis Moland.* Paris, 1876.

GHERARDI (EVARISTO) *Le Théâtre Italien de Gherardi, ou le recueil général de toutes les comédies et scènes Françoises jouées par les comédiens Italiens du Roi pendant tout le temps qu'ils ont été au service.* Edition nouvelle revue avec beaucoup d'exactitude. Paris, 6 Vols., 1717.

JAL (AUGUSTE) *Dictionnaire critique de Biographie et d'Histoire, errata et supplément pour tous les dictionnaires historiques d'après des documents authentiques inédits.* Paris, 1867.

MENAGE (GILLES) *Ménagiana, ou bon-mots, rencontres agréables, pensées judicieuses, et observations curieuses, de M. Ménage.* Amsterdam, 1693.

MOLAND (LOUIS) *Molière et la comédie italienne.* Paris, 1867.

RASI (LUIGI) *I Comici italiani. Biografia, bibliografia, iconografia.* Florence, 2 Vols., 1897—1905.

RICCOBONI (LUIGI) *Histoire de l'ancien théâtre italien depuis la decadence de la comédie latine, avec un catalogue des tragédies et comédies italiennes imprimées depuis l'an* 1500 *jusqu'à l'an* 1650, *et une dissertation sur la tragédie moderne.* Paris, 2 Vols., 1728—31.

SAND (MAURICE) *Masques et Bouffons* (*Comédie italienne*). Paris, 2 Vols., 1860.

Calendar of State Papers, Domestic Series, of the reign of Charles II. Edited by M. A. E. Green and F. H. Blackburne Daniell.

Calendar of Treasury Books of the reign of Charles II. Edited by W. A. Shaw.

The BIRTH, LIFE *and* DEATH *of*

SCARAMOUCH

TO

HER ROYAL HIGHNESS
MADAME
LA DUCHESSE D'ORLEANS

MADAME,

It is no small labour to compose an Epistle Dedicatory for personages of so high a rank and such great merit as YOUR ROYAL HIGHNESS.

It is a task wherein the whole Academy, be it ever so capable, would have trouble to succeed, and it is a rock on which a thousand people are wrecked every day. MADAME, *I most humbly pray you to approve that of all the formalities of a Dedication I shall observe only that one which obliges me to be concise and to express myself with as much brevity as respect,*

YOUR ROYAL HIGHNESS'S

most humble, most obedient,

and most respectful servant,

ANGELO CONSTANTINI, *called* MEZZETIN.

d

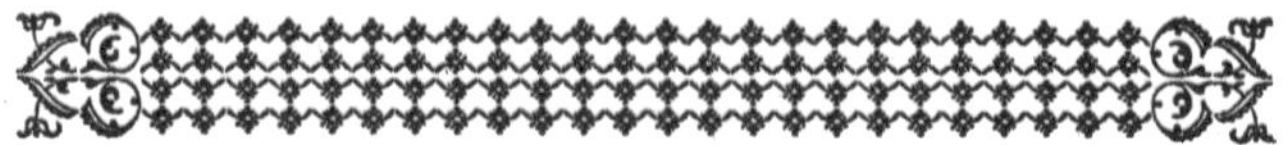

THE COMIC MUSE

PRESENTS

MEZZETIN

TO HER ROYAL HIGHNESS

MADAME

LA DUCHESSE D'ORLEANS

PRINCESS, I dare be sure of this,
  That Comedy by Quip and Wile
Entices you with richer Bliss
  Than Tragedy's ambitious Style.

True, your Heroic Heart delights
  When antique Heroes hold the Scene,
And hardly stoops from those bold Flights
  To mark my Jests among the Mean.

Yet, maugre this, as true I prove,
  The Buskin sometime sulking lies,
That I your Laughter oft'ner move
  Than my grand Sister doth your Sighs.

Ah, my poor Scaramouch, who won
The Crown of all the acting Race!
How many a Time his Wit and Fun
Brought to your Lips the smiling Grace!

Into the Night that hath no End
Had he who wore the Sock so well
Vanish'd, but Mezzetin his Friend
His Ways and Days stor'd up to tell.

That with your glorious Name his Book
May now go forth, this Friend doth pray,
And, Madam, in your Mien and Look
I scan your Pleasure, Yea or Nay.

I bring the Author trembling here
Awaiting what you will declare;
Come, Mezzetin, put off your Fear,
Her Majesty smiles on your Prayer.

STANZAS

WHICH MEZZETIN had the honour of reciting before her ROYAL HIGHNESS, in offering her his LIFE OF SCARAMOUCH.

PRINCESS whom all Observers view
  To shine with Royal Beauties, deign
A pause to hear th' Affair in few,
Ere you fall laughing might and main.

Now Mezzetin, as you must know,
  Though small his Greek and Latin Skill—
Rather a-hunting he would go—
  Has clambered up Parnassus Hill.

Yes, Lady, I—it is no Joke—
  I stand upon that very Peak ;
This Book you honour'd, I invoke,
  To witness, it's the Truth I speak.

Why, what a wondrous Transformation,
  From Huntsman, bless me, and from Play'r,
As great in Rhyme as in Narration—
  Hey, a Historian takes the Air !

Lord knows how many a scribbling Quorum
  Will dart their Vollies through my Book!
But I don't give a Penny for 'em,
  If 't pleases you therein to look.

Would you, for Scaramouch's Sake
  But speak in Favour, very soon
The most uncouth of 'em would quake
  Nor dare let loose e'en one Lampoon.

For Cabbages fam'd Alexander
  Used to swap Kingdoms once of old;
The Bus'ness prov'd Advantage slender;
  Tons on his Hands were left unsold.

And if To-Day your Int'rest meet
  The trifling Present which I bring
And give the Blessing I entreat,
  You'll far outdo that fabled King.

PREFACE

SCARAMOUCH has been so often in the thoughts of Playgoers, and his memory is still held in such high esteem, that it is needless to remind the Reader of the honour invariably paid to this celebrated Player. I shall remark only that he justly merited the reputation he had acquired and that he was one of the most skilful Mimes the last centuries have seen.

I accord him this qualification because after the pattern of the ancient Mimes he expressed the plot by poses and gestures rather than by words, which should be the aim of every Player, for everyone knows that *Segnius irritant animos demissa per aures, quam quæ sunt oculis subjecta fidelibus.*[1] *Scaramouch*, then, was not content merely to let the Spectator hear what he wished to say, he even made his words take shape before his eyes, so great was his talent for uniting speech to gesture. It may be said that every part of him had a tongue, his feet, his hands, his head, and

[1] Those things conveyed through the ears are understood less quickly than those witnessed by the assiduous eyes.

that his least gesture was the fruit of meditation. Hence, without enquiring whether History owes more to Heroes, since their mighty deeds are the reason for its being, or whether Heroes are more indebted to History, because it preserves their achievements for posterity, I venture to submit that the public to whom I am so greatly obliged will be deeply grateful to me for having brought to life again a man who during his existence was universally admired.

Let none expect to find in this little Book an Historical Novel or a Comical Romance; I have neither sufficient time nor skill to undertake a Work of that nature. I leave such subjects to those who have composed works on such people as the *Ildegartes*, the *Maries de Bourgogne* and the *Ducs de Guise Balafrés*. Besides I should be loth to impose on the Reader, and my Hero is, if I may so style him, too modern for me to presume to take the same liberty these gentlemen have taken.

Neither have I desired to imitate that Author who under the specious title of *Arlequiniana* [1] sold to the public stories which the late *Domenico* would have . . . rather than have even thought of tiring those with whom he had the honour to

[1] Written by Charles Cotolendi (1694). A collection of anecdotes—said to be untrue—regarding the celebrated Harlequin Domenico Biancolelli (1640–1688).

converse. I have striven then to set forth in the simplest language in my power the deeds of *Scaramouch* which I had from his own lips. That is, my dear Reader, all that I desired to say in this Preface, the reading of which I gladly would have spared you if by suppressing it I had not lessened this small Volume still more.

SCARAMOUCH having departed for Italy, a rumour arose that he had been drowned in the Rhône, which afforded Loret occasion to devise the following Verses in his praise. Although this Poem, which may be termed the Funeral Ode of Scaramouch, displays a little of the spirit of Burlesque which then dominated the votaries of Parnassus, I thought that the Reader would not be displeased to see it.

O ALL ye Courtiers and ye Cits
Who patronize the Tribe of Wits,
O all ye Lovers of the Stage
Which I myself declare's the Rage,
Break forth in Groans, in Tears, in Sighs,
In Blusterings, Mutt'rings, and loud Cries,
Fall into gen'ral doleful Dumps,
Your Breasts bemaul with leaden Thumps,
Become the Images of Care,
Snatch out your Whiskers and your Hair,
Tear at your Faces with your Nails,
Forget all Pleasure's tasteless Tales,
With loud Revilings Fate upbraid,
For Scaramouch the Great is dead.
A Man of an unrivalled Quality
In the rare Art of Whimsicality,
Who mimicked with a marv'lous Knack
Both Woeful Will and Random Jack,

Ignoramuses, Logicians,
In brief, all Sorts and all Conditions ;
So that, the simple Truth t' express,
This unapproach'd Resourcefulness
In all Theatric Enterprize
Excelled all his Contemp'raries.
To end, this Lord of Jubilation
And Theme of all Men's Conversation
If Rumour we for once believe,
On the Rhône's Bank of Life took Leave,
A Flood came down with sudden Wrath
And caught him helpless on his Path,
Down in a hollow Vale and Swamp
And quenched at once his Life's bright Lamp.
I was his Friend, and much have grieved
To be of such a Man bereav'd ;
I in my Sorrow thus have penned
An Epitaph upon this Friend.

EPITAPH

Mourn, though no Lady Isabeau
  Lies in this melancholy Tomb,
Nor holy Maid is here below,
  But Comedy's lost Rose and Bloom ;
The Heaven has but a single Sun,
Earth had one Scaramouch, but One.

When he was here and at his best
  His Genius pleas'd on ev'ry Side,
But still the Nobles lov'd his Jest
  Above the Mob ; and far and wide
" The Prince of Wits " the Man was nam'd,
" The Wit of Princes " also claim'd.

Then let us, in the Place of Flow'rs,
  Let fall our Tears upon his Grave,
My Sighs tell true my Sorrow's Pow'rs,
  For that I need no Pardon crave ;
Well may he now receive our Tears
Who made us laugh for Years and Years.

THE tidings of Scaramouch's death being proved false, this same Loret made these other Verses, in the same manner as those previous.

LITTLE and great ones, young ones, old ones,
Whose Hearts are anything but cold ones,
Who scarce would rather rule the Earth
Than sit and hear the Sons of Mirth,
Your Moans and Sighs no longer urge
And your dull Melancholy purge,
(Cassia and Rhubarb you are spar'd),
Give over plucking at your Beard,
Put all your Troubles in a Sack,
Your Chests no longer Thump and Thwack;
Make no more Mouths at Destiny,
Your Cheeks henceforth should scratchless be.
Waste no more Shouts upon the Wind,
Leave Squalls and Murm'rings all behind,
Of those Pallid Looks repent,
Like the Masks abroad in Lent;
Hector not Dame Destiny,
But reveal your Gaiety,
Make your Entertainment plain;
Scaramouch is back again,
And the story of his Fate
Which had made me desolate
Was a Bubble and a Fiction
And has met its Contradiction.
With much Trouble in my Time
I have brought back to their Prime
Many Men thought dead and buried.

Yet, my Muse, I dare aver it,
Never have I to Life restor'd
In Book or Play, by Pen or Word,
A Heart so good, mere Truth to vouch,
So good and great as Scaramouch.

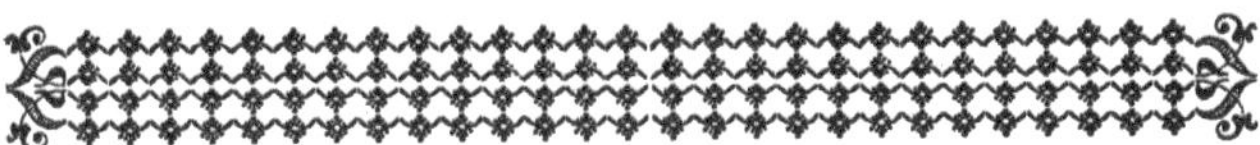

EPIGRAM

ON THE PORTRAIT OF SCARAMOUCH

SHALL we upon de Troye or Mignard call
To paint the Copy of th' Original
Who out of Italy amongst us came ?
I do no Wrong to those rare Artists' Fame,
When I despair to see their Skill renew
What Nature's self found she could barely do.

THE BIRTH, LIFE AND DEATH OF SCARAMOUCH

CHAPTER I

Of the Birth of Scaramouch

TIBERIO FIORILLI, known as *Scaramouch*, was born at *Naples* in the year one thousand six hundred and eight. His Father, who was a Captain of Horse, desiring to marry a second time, wished to espouse one of his Cousins who resided in the town of *Capua*, but could never obtain the Bishop's permission on account of the nearness of kin.

He disputed this matter at great length with this Prelate's brother, who, on beginning to join banter with argument, so aroused his temper that without any more ado he passed his sword through his body and killed him.

The Father of our *Scaramouch* being obliged to leave the Kingdom of *Naples* to escape the fruits of his action and finding himself in a strange Country with neither money nor any other employment than that of looking after his two Children, was forced, although a Nobleman, to play the Charlatan and sell quack Medicines.

Scaramouch, his second Son, was much more trouble to him than *Trapolin* the elder one, because when still at the breast he every day sucked dry the bosoms of two wet-nurses, and became so large an eater when grown up, that it was all the difficulty in the world to satisfy him. He filched Nostrums from his Father and what was priced at thirty sols[1] he gave away for ten to the Tavern-keepers and Bakers to procure bread and wine. His Father being apprised of it, beat him with a stick and drove him out of doors. He was then eighteen years old but, despite his youth, he did not lack spirit, and his one regret at leaving his Father's house was to find himself without money and in possession of a very large appetite.

CHAPTER II

How Scaramouch conducted himself at Rome

SCARAMOUCH having arrived at *Rome* just in the month of December when the Northerly Wind is felt more keenly there than

[1] A *sol* or *sou* was originally the twentieth part of a *livre,* and is now the name of the French halfpenny, which is the twentieth part of a *franc.*

in any other part of *Italy*, and as he had only a short silk cloak which hardly covered his buttocks, began to seek means of protecting himself against his two deadliest enemies, hunger and cold.

Having planted himself for this purpose right up against a Tobacco Merchant's shop in the *Piazza Navona*, he begged a pinch of Snuff from everyone who entered the shop, and putting four fingers and thumb into their snuff-boxes, took out enough to fill a small calabash which he held under his cloak.

After having made, during the day, a powder of Orange Flowers, Neroli, Bergamot and Jessamine, he resold it in the evening at a low price to the same Merchant who, seeing the mixture that *Scaramouch* had contrived, called it Snuff *Mille Fleurs*.

One of the Pope's *Swiss* Guards, having bought Snuff at the same shop, came out holding his box in his hands. *Scaramouch*, in his usual manner, went to take the Snuff, but the *Swiss*, feeling offended at his conduct, began to be furiously angry with him, calling him *Schelme*[1] many times and threatening him with his fist.

Scaramouch exhausted himself in endeavouring to gain his pardon, making the most grotesque movements with his hand and his whole body ; upon which the *Swiss*, seeing in this only

[1] Knave, swindler.

a further affront, gave him several blows with the staff of his Halberd, tearing his cloak and severely bruising his shoulders. Little pleased with the incivility of the *Swiss* and fearing, moreover, even more unfortunate sequels to his little trade, he abandoned *Rome* and went to *Civita Vecchia*.

CHAPTER III

How Scaramouch tricked two Turkish Slaves from the Pope's Galleys

WHEN he had arrived in that town, he went for a walk on the Quay, whereupon, seeing two *Turkish* Slaves who were counting over a sum of money which they had gained by their toil, he cut a piece from the fore-part of his shirt and adroitly put it in place of the linen which served the Slaves to wrap up their money. He contrived this so well that the *Turks*, suspecting nothing, replaced their money in the piece of linen they found to hand.

As they were about to go away, *Scaramouch*, who had gone to sleep in the sun some paces from them, pretending to awake with a start, began to cry out: "Alas! Alas! I am done for, they have robbed me. Justice! Justice! Thief! Thief!" He held them by their sleeves and as

Archers and *Sbirri*[1] were not lacking in that Country, all three were taken immediately before a Judge.

Scaramouch accused the two Slaves of having stolen his money which he had put in a corner of his shirt. The Judge having questioned him as to the number and value of the pieces which had been stolen from him, he answered so truly in every particular, showing the fore-part of his shirt, that the Judge, never doubting the truth of the matter, sentenced the *Turks* to give back the money to him, and further had them beaten for Thieves.

After this affair *Scaramouch*, recollecting that he was a Nobleman born, dressed himself magnificently, and with a Servant at his heels, took the road for *Lombardy*.

CHAPTER IV

How Scaramouch was sent to the Galleys after being robbed by his Servant

ON the way *Scaramouch*, conversing with his Man, bethought himself, unwisely enough, to confide to him the reason he had left his Father, the misfortune that had happened to him in *Rome*, and the trick he had played on the two Slaves.

[1] Italian police.

In the evening, as they arrived at a Hostelry near the main road, he denied himself nothing, so eager was he to satisfy his ravenous appetite, and ate and drank so well that they were forced to carry him from the table to his bed. It was not long before he began to snore like one of the largest organ pipes.

The Servant, seeing his Master so deep in sleep, that all the Cannons in the Arsenal could not have awakened him, drew his breeches from beneath his pillow, and seizing the rest of his gear, suddenly decamped by a window which gave on to the back of the house.

Poor *Scaramouch*, finding himself on awakening as naked as a rat, saw the truth of the Proverb *lightly come, lightly go*. It was no use his shouting, swearing and raging, for at the end he had to bear his loss patiently, since the mischief was beyond remedy.

The Landlord, out of charity, gave him a Slave's sorry smock to cover himself with and let him stay another night out of pity. The next day, *Scaramouch* repaid his kindness before going, by robbing him of his kitchen chain, which was made not unlike a Galley slave's chain, and pursued his way to *Ancona* asking alms from everyone he met.

" In the name of the most holy and adorable Trinity," he said to them, " show your charity to a poor Slave, lately rescued from the hands of the *Turks*, who has suffered an infinity of tortures for the confession of his faith." He accompanied these words with such touching gestures and so great a profusion of tears, that few could deny him, and he found this manner of living so profitable that doubtless he never would have quitted it so soon if it had not been for the misfortune which happened to him in the town of *Ancona*.

I do not know by what chance there happened to be at this time in the Harbour three Galleys from *Naples*. Be it as it may, one day the Officer in charge of the Slaves seeing *Scaramouch* in his Slave's habit, laid his hand on his collar and cried: "How now, you rascal! How now, you villain! did you think then thus to escape from Justice? But, thank God, I have found you, you gallows bird! you vile wretch!" It was of no use for *Scaramouch* to raise his eyes to Heaven and to protest loudly his innocence, and the Officer did not hesitate to take him on board one of the Galleys in the full sight of everyone, where, having given him the *bastonnado*, he put him with the other Slaves.

The Captain of the Galley having arrived a little later, the Officer informed him that by a fortunate chance, he had recovered the *Neapolitan* Slave who had taken flight with five others two months before. The Captain was eager to see him and at first thought he greatly resembled the *Neapolitan* Slave who had escaped. But, having recognised by his voice that it was not him he sought, he set him at liberty, and gave him some silver pieces to soften the blows he had received.

Scaramouch, seeing the danger he had run of being bound to an oar for life, promptly went to a Jew's shop to buy a suit and forsook, though not without regret, the profession of mendicant Slave.

CHAPTER V

How Scaramouch entered a Company of Players

HAVING bought a habit according to his small means, *Scaramouch* went from *Ancona* into a town of the *Romagna*, called *Fanno*, where he found a Company of very tattered Players. Although he had never before set foot on a Stage, he presented himself and boldly informed them that he was an excellent Player, as if he had foreseen what one day he would become.

The Players received him with joy and having asked him what character he intended to perform, he told them that he played Comedy under the name of *Scaramouch*, and that he would dress himself in such and such a manner. They discovered as much oddity in the name as in the costume ; and this Person with reason appeared extraordinary to them, since of his kind, *Scaramouch* has proved to be an original which up to the present has never had a copy and perhaps never will have any.

He was asked further in what Piece he wished to play: he chose *Le Festin de Pierre*, which he esteemed above all the others on account of the eating there is in it.

This Piece then was announced with a new Actor. Curiosity attracted an extraordinary crowd, and *Scaramouch* having succeeded perfectly during the course of the Play, did his duty by the Repast so well that he thought to burst in the midst of the applause.

The Public were so delighted by his first Performance that they clamoured for a second, to which *Scaramouch* willingly consented, and in place of the hard-boiled eggs with which he had stuffed himself the first time, he ate a large turkey, two pheasants and a pigeon pie.

He restored this company to a thriving condition and he who had never before set foot on a Stage was regarded by his Fellows as the greatest man in the world, and they found in his person all the facetious humour of *Plautus* and sometimes even the majestic gravity of *Terence*.

It is true that *Scaramouch* was not greatly attached to the Study of Books, but on the other hand he was endowed with such intelligence that he appeared wise despite his never having learned anything.

This troupe went to pass the Carnival at *Mantua*, and after three or four performances *Scaramouch* so greatly pleased the Prince that he was not long without receiving some considerable tokens of his liberality, and I leave it to be imagined whether *Scaramouch*, who was naturally disposed to avarice, knew how to profit by the occasion.

CHAPTER VI

How Scaramouch obtained a Suit of Clothes and a Horse from the Duke of Mantua

SCARAMOUCH going one day to wait on the Duke, told him that he had a fine Play in mind but lacked the Costumes necessary to perform it. The Duke at once gave orders that he should be allowed to take from his Wardrobe whatever he needed.

According to the Prince's Commands, he took for himself a Suit of black velvet, embroidered with seed-pearls ; and besides that, he took a set of rich horse-trappings. When he appeared on the Stage in this magnificent Dress, a Player remarked that a great Prince must have lent it to him. He replied :—" What do you mean by lent, Scoundrel ? Do you take a Prince for a Dealer in old Clothes? Say rather that he gave it me and you will speak sensibly."

As a matter of fact, the Duke did give it to him after the Comedy and *Scaramouch*, desiring to thank him, made such an amusing pretence of being embarrassed in his compliments that the whole Assembly thought to choke with laughter. Some while afterwards *Scaramouch*, mounted on an ass, went to meet the Duke arrayed in the dress and displaying the fine harness he had given him. The Prince, astonished at this extravagance, inquired the reason for it. He replied that it was to show all the world the beautiful presents with which his Highness had honoured him, and if he had possessed money enough he would not have failed to buy a beautiful horse to correspond with the splendid trappings. The Duke, understanding at once, commanded his Master of the Horse to give him immediately one from his own stables.

Soon after *Scaramouch* sold it to a great Lord who had envied it. This having come to the Prince's ears our Player said to him in apology, that he had only parted with it in order to please him, for if he had kept that mettlesome horse much longer, he undoubtedly would have broken his neck, or at least injured some limb; which would have grieved His Highness. This Prince, who was very fond of *Scaramouch*, good-naturedly accepted his excuses and only with much ado accorded him leave to go to *Bologna the Wealthy* where he had longed to be for some time past.

CHAPTER VII

How Scaramouch was put in Prison and what he did to revenge himself on the Provost-Marshal

WHEN *Scaramouch* had arrived at *Bologna*, which is the usual meeting-place of Comedians during Lent, he saw himself esteemed by some but envied by many others, which generally happens to those who have distinguished themselves by their merit.

As he did not despise the fair sex, he soon took a Mistress with whom he delighted in walking every evening in the Moon-light ; this was not without opposition on the Lady's part, who knew the danger to which she exposed herself in remaining in the streets at unseasonable hours contrary to the strict orders of the Police. But *Scaramouch*, relying on his sword and his courage, mocked her fears. However, notwithstanding all his bravery, the *Barigel* or Provost-Marshal accompanied by ten or twelve *Sbirri*, meeting with them, seized upon *Scaramouch* and his Mistress and carried them to Prison. *Scaramouch* was released the next day on paying a fine of ten pistoles [1] and a like sum for his Mistress, but he swore to be revenged for it.

One day of the great Festival, the Provost-Marshal, followed by thirty Archers, having gone to Mass at *Notre Dame de la Mort*, *Scaramouch*, having found an opportunity to come close to him in the press, cut off the jewelled buttons attached to the back of his scarlet mantle and then, without being perceived, made his way out of the Church.

The Provost-Marshal, having returned home, was extremely surprised at the boldness of the person who had cut off his buttons and made every attempt to discover him. To this end he caused to be arrested a great number of Cut-purses, of whom he whipped some and sent others to the Galleys ; but all to no purpose.

Scaramouch, who still did not consider himself sufficiently revenged, dressed himself as a Journeyman-Tailor and, learning that the Provost-Marshal was detained on business with the Cardinal Legate, went boldly to his house, holding Scissors in one hand and the stolen Buttons in the other. In this guise he spoke to the Provost-Marshal's wife, whom he told that the Gentleman, having found his Buttons, had sent him to take his mantle and sew them on again.

[1] A pistole is the name given to the quarter doubloon of Spain and worth approximately sixteen shillings pre-war.

The good Lady did not hesitate a moment to carry out her husband's supposed orders.

No sooner had *Scaramouch* the mantle than he could not refrain from sharing his joy with his Mistress and to confide to her the trick he had played. But having reflected afterwards that he had disclosed his secret to a woman who would have difficulty in keeping it, for fear of running into further disgrace, as well as not to be obliged to pay some little arrears he owed his Mistress, he departed without taking leave of her and withdrew to *Florence*.

CHAPTER VIII

How Scaramouch was received by the Grand Duke of Florence

ON the road to Florence, a Nobleman having asked *Scaramouch* who he was, he called himself *Fredonelli* and said that he was Musician to the Viceroy of *Naples*. The Nobleman, finding something extraordinary and at the same time pleasing in *Scaramouch's* features, deemed that he would be well adapted to entertain the Duke of *Florence*.

As soon as they arrived at this town, he informed this Prince that a celebrated Musician had come with him and perhaps he would not be displeased to listen to him. *Scaramouch* was called and without waiting to be asked twice, began to improvise daintily on his guitar and then sang the comic Song which I set here for the benefit of those who heard him sing.

L'Asinello innamorato
Canta, è raggia â tutte l'hore.
Pare un Musico affamato,
Quando narra il suo dolore,
E cantando d'amor va,
Ut re mi fa sol la. (He brays.)

Quando vede l'Asinella
Canta, all'hor con vocce acuta,
Pare un Maestro di Capella,
Quando batte la battuta :
E cantando d'amor va,
Ut re mi fa sol la. (He brays.)

Se tal'hor é nella stalla,
Mai fatica non lo doma,
Sempre salta & sempre balla,
Quando porta anco la soma,
E cantando d'amor va,
Ut re mi fa sol la. (He brays.)

Scaramouch sang this Air so pleasantly and accompanied it with a Drollery so diverting that the Grand Duke held his sides for laughter. This Prince asked him to sing another Song which he did immediately, beginning this other about the Cat.

Amor che cossa ai fatto,
A far innamorar il mio bel Gatto,
Assé lo vo castrare,
Acciò lasci é non torni più ad amare,
Cossi sará di te disciolto é schiao,
Ne per Gatta fará più gnao gnao. (He mews.)

Sopra il ciel delle mura,
Piange il misero piange sua suentura,
E con signaolati accenti
Fa, che s'oda d'intorno i suoi lamenti,
Solo si lagna é sta fra il tetto è il trao,
Va parlando al suo ben dicendo gnao. (He mews.)

As he finished these words, the Duke ran to embrace him and vowed that never had anyone diverted him so well.

Scaramouch then discovered to the Grand Duke that he was a Player and that he wished to go and perform at *Naples*. This generous Prince ordered one hundred pistoles to be counted out to him, promised him his protection and further gave him Letters of Recommendation which *Scaramouch* made use of, as will be seen in the sequel.

CHAPTER IX

How Scaramouch made the Journey from Florence to Leghorn at the expense of two Jews

SCARAMOUCH having left *Florence*, encountered two men on horseback, of whom he enquired the road they were taking; they replied that they were going to *Leghorn*. He begged them to suffer him to be of their company because otherwise, being a stranger and not knowing the roads, he ran the risk of going astray. They joined with him the more willingly because in asking this courtesy he had made such grimaces that they could not keep from laughter.

While on the way, *Scaramouch* enquired who they were; they told him that one was called *Aaron* and the other *Mordecai*, and that they were *Jewish* Merchants living at *Leghorn*. Scaramouch being questioned in turn by the Merchants, as to his name and quality, replied that as to the latter, his only quality was that of an honest man, but that he was a *Portuguese*. His father was called *Don Juan Castillos* and himself *Pedro Castillo*, and both his Parents had lived a long while at *Lisbon*, like good Christians outwardly, but as true *Jews* in secret. He added that, having neither Father nor Mother, he was going to *Leghorn* to proclaim himself a *Jew*, and that, thank God, he had still sufficient substance to live nobly.

The *Jews*, delighted at hearing this, confirmed him in his design and exhorted him to take another name. He told them that since he had the good fortune to fall into their hands, he placed himself entirely under them in this matter.

The two *Jews*, having run through almost all the names in the Old Testament, gave him that of *Benjamin* and paid for him on the way; which *Scaramouch* made semblance of not wishing to suffer, and only permitted with great trouble, saying that he would settle with them at the end of the journey.

At a league from *Leghorn, Scaramouch* begged them to tell him of a lodging. *Aaron*, with a pleasant courtesy, offered him his own, saying that he was unmarried and that he could remain in it until he had found an apartment to his liking. *Scaramouch* would not accept this kindness except on condition that he paid so much a day. The *Jew*, who had all the characteristics of his race, condescended; to the great regret of *Scaramouch*, who was no less parsimonious although a Christian.

Arrived at *Leghorn* he went to lodge with *Aaron* who made him known to the Rabbis; they importuned him unceasingly to come to their Synagogue; but he always found some excuse, and then, when he could be alone, he used to go on the Quay to see if he could not find some ship about to set sail for *Naples*. At the end of a fortnight he fortunately found a Tartane[1] in which he secured a passage.

The difficulty was how to get away his valise from *Aaron's* house. After having considered the matter for a moment, this is the subterfuge which he employed. He sought out the Inquisitor and said to him: " Reverend Father, you must know that a certain *Jew* in the *Rue Neuve*, called *Aaron*, and his Cousin *Mordecai*, wish to force me to embrace their faith. They have laid hands on all my belongings and I dare not go near them for fear that they will keep me a prisoner. You know, Reverend Father, they are a people accursed by God. I have discharged all their expenses from *Florence* hither and they will not repay me the charges I have paid for them. I have secured my place on a Tartane that is going to *Naples* whither I must return immediately. Here are letters from the *Grand Duke* which will inform your reverence of the truth." In saying these words, he began to cry profusely, disconcerting the Inquisitor's gravity, who, seeing the letters, made the *Jews* come before him and, without even listening to them, ordered them to restore *Scaramouch* his valise and further to give him ten *Spanish* pistoles. *Scaramouch* thanked the Inquisitor and went off immediately to embark on the Tartane which left half-an-hour later.

[1] *Tartane,* a small two-masted boat with a lateen sail, common in the Mediterranean.

CHAPTER X

How Scaramouch contrived to live at the expense of two Monks during the voyage and of the artful manner in which he cheated them of a Gold Crucifix

SCARAMOUCH would still have had time enough to procure provisions, according to the custom of those who make voyages in big ships, because it is not easy to land. He, however, troubled little about buying anything, hoping that he would find means to live at the expense of his fellow-travellers.

Among the great company which he found on the Tartane there were two Monks on whom he cast his eyes, intending to live on them as far as *Naples*.

Hardly had the Tartane left the Quay than he began to intone the Litanies of the Saints, but in so pious a voice, that everyone was edified exceedingly by it, particularly the two good Fathers. When these prayers were finished he followed with the *Credo*, the *Salve* and the *De Profundis* after which, everyone having risen, he alone remained on his knees for above an hour, feigning to be in the most profound contemplation: but in reality all his meditations turned only on inventing a means of eating so that it cost him nothing.

The dinner hour approaching, one of these good Fathers came to interrupt and draw him from his profound ecstasies, to *Scaramouch's* great relief, who already beginning to be weary, asked nothing better than to join conversation with him. The good Father wished to commend his devotion, but *Scaramouch* modestly casting down his eyes, rejected his praises and told him in a bigoted way that he was a great sinner and had done more wickedness even than could be imagined.

While the passengers spread out their little stores of provisions, some on benches and others on chests, a Sailor came to serve dinner to the good Fathers in the sight of *Scaramouch.*

The one who had conversed with him having asked his name and country, he replied that he was the son of a Nobleman of *Naples*, eighty years old, who was worth nearly a hundred thousand crowns. As for himself, owing to his having been afflicted with a severe illness which had greatly enfeebled his sight, his Father who loved him fondly had dedicated him to the great Saint Anthony of *Padua* whence he was returning, paying his journey by soliciting alms, to fulfil his Father's vows ; and that which gave him most pain was to see himself forced to ask from others that which he could himself give, as he was very generous. He added further that since he was an only son, he had the design of becoming a

Monk as soon as he arrived at *Naples*, in gratitude for God's grace in giving him time to do penance.

Having listened to him with admiration, the good Father exhorted him to persevere and in a loud voice made known so beautiful and so pious a resolution. Everyone was so edified by it that each offered him his table. But the good Fathers begged him so earnestly to dine with them, that *Scaramouch* thanked the others for their goodwill, and said to the Reverend Father that he accepted so much more willingly the honour that they desired to do him, because he would be well content to begin to accustom himself to their manner of living.

In reality, he only accepted their invitation because he believed that his appetite would be the better satisfied. After he had sat down to table and put on his spectacles, to spare the Reverend Fathers the invitations which are customarily made to a guest, he devoured at first sight all that was put before him. One of these good Fathers wishing to ask him some questions during dinner, *Scaramouch*, who feared to miss a morsel, said to him: " My Reverend Fathers, God forbid that I should give you lessons, but I believe that it is meet to keep silence at mealtime since we shall have time enough to talk afterwards."

Seeing that the good Fathers ate no longer,

he got up from the table with tears in his eyes and his hands raised to Heaven. The Fathers wishing to know why he cried, he told them that it was for joy at having fallen into such good hands. But the real cause of his tears was due to his having seen removed a fat capon which he had not ventured to touch.

After having thanked the Monks, *Scaramouch* vowed to them on the honour of a Nobleman that, on arriving at *Naples*, they would receive an ample recompense for their charity; and that his Father, not having a long while to live, would bequeath all his wealth to their Convent.

One word leading to another, I know not how, the conversation turned on the town of *Rome*, in regard to which one of the Fathers said that the Pope had made him a gift of a gold Crucifix, which he esteemed not so much on account of its value (although it was worth fifty pistoles) as for its virtue to vanquish demons.

Hardly had he uttered these words when *Scaramouch* began to make the most frightful grimaces, rolling his eyes in his head and foaming at the mouth like a person possessed. He played his part so well that the Father, believing him to be troubled by an evil spirit, placed his gold cross on his stomach, which only served to make him more furious and give vent to howls, accompanied by uncouth words, which frightened the spectators.

Always moderating his transports little by little, he fell into a quieter condition and, as if he had awakened from a profound lethargy, he fell on his knees to thank his liberators, keeping nevertheless in his restless eyes some traces of the violent agitation from which he had suffered.

He could not leave off kissing the Crucifix, at the same time weighing it in his hand to judge if it was of the value reputed. At last, he begged the good Father to let it remain with him during the voyage, for fear that he might fall into a similar pass. But it was not without great trouble that he obtained the favour he besought.

When he saw himself provided with the holy relic, he made a thousand fabulous stories on his pretended possession. Sometimes the *Demon* had carried him to the top of a steeple, sometimes it had made him fast for a whole fortnight ; in short, he invented a new adventure every day.

As they passed *Ischia* and *Proschyta*, two little islands hard by *Naples*, many long-boats came alongside the Tartane to take off the passengers. While everyone was occupied in collecting his property, *Scaramouch*, with his valise under his arm, jumped nimbly into one of the boats, and pretending to be extremely hurried, made the men row so quickly that it was soon lost to sight.

Not finding *Scaramouch*, the Fathers learned,

but too late, of his escape. I leave to be imagined the Fathers' consternation as he carried away the beautiful Crucifix. It suffices to say that *Scaramouch* again found the secret of both living at others' expense and having in addition a piece of jewellery so precious as a cross worth fifty pistoles.

CHAPTER XI

How Scaramouch, having laid out all his money on fine feathers and rich living, returned to Comedy and attained the good graces of the Duc de Satrian

ARRIVED at *Naples*, *Scaramouch* dressed himself magnificently and hired a coach with two Footmen, and changing his Mistress almost every day, omitted nothing in order to give himself all the pleasures which can be had in a big town when one has money.

He soon squandered all that he amassed since he was in *Florence*, and finding nobody would lend him anything, the Neapolitans not being generous enough to be duped, he was obliged to dismiss his equipage, and saw himself reduced to the sad necessity of waiting on himself.

It is customarily said that " hunger will break through stone walls," so that want of money forced *Scaramouch* to put aside for the time being those thoughts of grandeur and nobility with which he was infatuated when he had his pockets well lined.

A Company of Players happening to be in the town of *Naples*, he went to ask if he could join it. He was received with pleasure, and as a member of it he played the part of *Scaramouch* so effectively that the *Duc de Satrian*, having heard the new Actor well spoken of, resolved to send for the Troupe to come to his Palace and entertain his family.

On the day appointed for this festivity a great number of the Nobility were according to custom at the *Duke's* Palace. *Scaramouch* performed marvels and drew so many praises upon himself as, comforting his soul, would have been capable of satisfying the appetite of any other Player: however, *Scaramouch* being seated at table according to the Duke's express command, proved himself so excellent a trencherman that it was soon realised that Glory was not the food he sought the most.

Besides, if in my description of another Repast I forget to observe that he acquitted himself finely of the duty of a large eater, I pray the Reader to suppose it said for the rest of this Story.

Supper finished, as each guest wished to return home, the Duke's men took silver Torches to light the company to the door.

Scaramouch, to make himself useful, also took one of them in each hand and going into the street, he carried his politeness so far as to conduct himself to his lodging.

The following day *Scaramouch* returning to sup with the Duke, said to him that his Treasurer merited a sharp reproof since, if he had wished, he could have carried away a goodly part of his silver plate the night before; but that he had contented himself with a pair of Torches which he would look after much better than his Officer, if it so pleased His Highness to give them to him.

The Prince indeed made him a present of them, but when he wished to depart, he ordered a Footman to conduct him, for fear it might cost him another two Torches if *Scaramouch* again lighted himself home.

CHAPTER XII

How Scaramouch played at the Duc de Castre's where he encountered the Monk from whom he stole the Crucifix

THE *Duc de Castre*, having learned of the trick which *Scaramouch* had played upon the *Duc de Satrian*, longed to see him and to this end sent for the Company of Players to appear before him; but this Prince's Treasurer, who knew how *Scaramouch* had comported himself at the *Duc de Satrian's* house, took care to keep a close watch over his plate.

After the collation, which was served in the garden, *Scaramouch*, in his Stage dress, went into a secluded avenue to rehearse some new Scenes. Believing himself unobserved, he practised the grimaces and postures necessary to his part while the Monk of the Tartane looked at him attentively from behind a palisade.

This good Father having had plenty of time to examine him, after being a long time in doubt, was convinced at last that he whom he saw was the one formerly possessed with evil spirits. The Monk softly approached him from behind, and having caught him by his short mantle, asked for his Crucifix.

Scaramouch, who was not a little surprised to see himself recognised, all the same did not neglect to pretend to ignore the fact; but the more obstinately he denied it, the more his speech confirmed the Monk in his suspicions; it was no use his saying that he was a man of honour, that he was called *Scaramouch*, and that he was mistaken for another, the good Father did not yield and always holding him by his mantle began to shout with all his might "Thief! Thief!"

Foreseeing clearly that someone would come to the Father's help, *Scaramouch* broke away so quickly from his grasp that the people who ran from all sides towards the noise, found only the Monk holding *Scaramouch's* cloak.

The Duke and the Company having enquired the reason for his alarm, the Father recounted the manner in which *Scaramouch* had cheated him of his Crucifix on the voyage from *Leghorn* to *Naples*, and how having recognised him in the garden, he had seized him, but that he had escaped, leaving his mantle in his hands.

The story of this adventure made a great stir because *Scaramouch* had traversed the whole town in his Stage costume, not without drawing the whole population after him, and quickly packing his chest he embarked on a Vessel which was preparing to set sail for the Isle of *Malta*, reckoning himself very fortunate at having escaped so cheaply.

CHAPTER XIII

How the Captain's Mistress became enamoured of Scaramouch

SCARAMOUCH, now on board, was not long in making the acquaintance of the Captain who offered him a place at his own table, which filled *Scaramouch* with joy, and, being unaccustomed to refuse such invitations, he accepted wholeheartedly.

A *Spanish* lady, who also ate with the Captain, found *Scaramouch* much to her liking. His appearance and pleasant manners, joined to his fine figure, so greatly charmed her that she became madly in love with him and confided her secret to the Slave who waited upon her.

Scaramouch, on his side, soon perceived the tendency of her thoughts by the amorous glances which she cast on him at every moment, and he was completely confirmed in his opinion when the Slave whispered in his ear that her Mistress wished very much to speak with him.

He did not fail to profit by the occasion and one day, leaving the Captain on the Quarter-deck, he glided below into the Lady's cabin who eagerly welcomed him.

He had hardly commenced to enjoy his good fortune when all at once a great storm arose and was like to sink the Ship. The lady, troubled by the cries of the Sailors and the noise of the waves which she heard, roughly pushed him away, telling him that he was the cause of the danger.

The squall having lasted a few minutes at most, *Scaramouch*, who was standing against the cabin door, all confused and almost speechless, plucked up courage when he heard the *Spaniard* calling to him " *Mi Coracon, mis Oios, mi Alma, vengas, Senor Tiberio, vengas.*" [1] There was no

[1] "My heart, my eyes, my soul, come, Señor Tiberio, come."

need for her to call him twice, but while he tasted all that is sweetest in love, a tempest more violent than the former again interrupted the course of his pleasures.

Scaramouch, greatly to his sorrow, saw himself forced to leave the lady for a second time; he went on Deck whence the Captain had already thrown into the sea a great quantity of goods so as to lighten his Vessel.

Daybreak, having brought calm on the waters, stirred up great trouble in *Scaramouch's* breast, who, failing to discover his box, began to swear against the Captain and curse the pleasures he had enjoyed during the night with the *Spanish* lady.

The Captain, downcast at the loss of his cargo, and understanding from *Scaramouch's* imprecations that the *Spanish* lady had not been cruel to him, vented all his wrath on his rival and having nearly beaten him to death, landed him on a rocky and deserted coast.

Poor *Scaramouch*, reduced to this miserable plight, began to cry like a child, but seeing that he had no remedy for his ill-fortune, bestirred himself so well that after having climbed like a goat for over two hours, he reached the top of the Cliff.

CHAPTER XIV

How Scaramouch encountered a Company of Bandits who forced him to join them

DESTINY, which seemed to take delight in persecuting *Scaramouch*, caused him unhappily to fall into the hands of a Band of Highway Robbers who, taking him for a spy of the Viceroy of *Palermo*, questioned him with a Dagger at his throat.

Scaramouch who had never found himself in a similar situation, sought to calm them by all manner of the most humiliating postures, for fear deprived him of speech.

The Bandits paying no heed to his grimaces, he was forced to relate artlessly his whole adventure to them, but the Thieves disbelieving him, compelled him to follow them everywhere.

One day, these Bandits, having murdered a rich Merchant, from whom they took six hundred pistoles, wished to go and divide the plunder in a house which had long been uninhabited on account of the belief that it was haunted.

Three travellers who, a little while before, had come to take shelter in it, being frightened at the appearance of so many armed men and wishing to hide in the remotest corners, caused some plaster to fall; which noise terrified the Thieves who, in the belief that all the legions of Hell were about to be unloosed on them, took to flight leaving behind their money. Delighted at seeing them decamp, the travellers shut themselves in to divide the spoil.

At a musket shot from the place they had quitted so hurriedly, the Thieves beginning to bewail their money, compelled *Scaramouch* to return to see what had become of it.

Scaramouch not daring to refuse this task, however dangerous it appeared to him, arrived at the door of the house just as one of the travellers was saying to his comrades that Heaven had sent them this money just in time, since they had hardly fifteen sols when this good fortune came to them.

Having only half-heard these words, *Scaramouch* hastily returned to tell the Thieves that he had found the door shut, and that the Demons had come in such numbers that they had hardly fifteen sols apiece of all the money they had left them.

Although *Scaramouch* had a sufficiently easy conscience, as already may have been observed, he could not rid himself of his horror at being in the company of these Brigands, and would willingly have separated from them if he had not feared to be killed at the least semblance of his wishing to escape.

He cooked their meals and waited on them, but his greatest concern was when the Bandits changed their hiding-place; because he was loaded with all the baggage under which he thought, more than once, to be overwhelmed.

In changing their abode so frequently the thieves hoped to avoid the Provost-Marshal, but it happened just on the contrary that, owing to these continual changes, they fell into an ambuscade of more than thirty Archers who brought down five or six at the first volley, when all the rest ran away except *Scaramouch*, who was made prisoner.

He was taken to *Palermo*, bound hand and foot like a common Highway Robber, and he would have been hanged without trial, if the Judge, who wished to learn from his lips the number of the Thieves, had not stayed his execution.

On being questioned, *Scaramouch* related the manner in which the Bandits had forced him to follow them ; but this would have availed him little in his defence, if he had not remembered the name of the Captain who had landed him among the Mountains.

As it was not long since the selfsame Captain, who was called *Peresso*, had put into the port of *Palermo* to make an Inventory of the goods which he had been obliged to throw overboard, the Judge confronted him with two *Palermitan* merchants who, not daring to expose themselves any longer to the mercy of the sea, had left the vessel of the said *Peresso*.

They recognised *Scaramouch* and affirmed the truth of his statement; and the Judge having heard their depositions discharged him as innocent.

Scaramouch was beside himself with joy at being delivered from such a ticklish situation; however, his delight was greatly lessened when he saw himself penniless and that the most grasping of Jailors demanded another fifty carlini[1] to let him leave the Prison.

Not knowing which way to turn, *Scaramouch* sent to beg one of the Comedians who played in the Viceroy's Palace to have the kindness to help him. Although the members of this Troupe had never heard of his talents, they did not hesitate to release him charitably from Prison and even took him into their service for a testoon[2] a day.

Having served some time as a Supernumerary, *Scaramouch* offered to play an Interlude in the Comedy, which he would not have obtained had not the actor who played the Mask of Coviello happened to die.

Scaramouch had no sooner appeared on the Stage than he delighted the entire audience as usual until his comrades, who were the most

[1] A *carlino* was a small silver coin originally worth fourpence, first struck by Charles d'Anjou, King of Naples.

[2] A French coin of the 16th century worth about ten *sous*, so called from the head on its obverse.

skilful Players in all *Italy*, became jealous of him; they sought even to annoy him by preventing him from playing as often as he wished, but *Scaramouch* could not forget the kindly manner in which his fellows had succoured him, and reminding himself that if it had not been for them, he would perhaps have been rotting in Prison, he endured patiently all the vexations they put upon him.

This example of modesty and gratitude in a Player such as *Scaramouch*, should make blush with shame those who, thinking themselves more talented than their fellows, despise the whole Company of which they are part and in which they alone claim to decide everything.

CHAPTER XV

How Scaramouch fell in love with Marinette, his First Wife

HAVING made a serious reflection on the troubles brought upon him by his extravagance, *Scaramouch* began to turn more economical, and instead of squandering his substance in the Taverns on the days when he did not perform, he amused himself by going for a walk.

One day, when he was about a league from the Town, he saw a young girl drying her hair which she had just washed by the river-side and which was of so extraordinary a length that, although she was standing on a large stone, it still reached to the ground ; moreover it was of the most beautiful colour in the world.

This charming head of hair, added to the beauty of the young person whom it adorned, was a bond that fettered *Scaramouch's* heart.

The young blonde's Mother, seeing him so greatly taken by her Daughter, could not help remarking that he apparently found her greatly to his taste, since he looked at her so attentively.

He replied that truly he had never seen anyone so charming and that her Daughter was worthy of the admiration of the most fastidious connoisseurs.

The Mother, gathering from his discourse that he was enamoured of her Daughter, told him that she was seeking a husband and that, if he were single, it did not rest with the girl whether such a marriage should take place. " My husband," she added, " was an excellent Merchant whose death greatly injured our affairs, but if we have lacked plenty we have always lived as befits honest folk."

During this speech, *Scaramouch* maintained a preoccupied silence, and the Mother having enquired the reason of it, he replied that it was needful to ponder a long while on that which one should do only once ; and besides, he had heard it said that to secure a good wife, she must be without eyes, so as not to see her husband's amours, without a tongue, so as to be unable to reply when he quarrels with her, and lastly, without ears, so as not to hear a lover's flowery speeches.

" All the same, your Daughter appears to be neither blind, nor deaf nor dumb but, on the contrary, she has a neat foot and a charming countenance."

This discourse made the Mother laugh who said to *Scaramouch*, that she knew of no other fault in her Daughter than that of being poor. " So much the better," he replied, " it is a bad bargain when a Daughter must be given money to get rid of her. I shall marry yours without a dowry and only for the love that I bear her ; her beauty and her virtue will take the place of the greatest riches." While speaking thus on the proposed marriage, he escorted them to their house. He did not delay in making enquiries in the neighbourhood and, finding that the Mother had told him nothing that was not true, he married the girl at the end of a fortnight.

CHAPTER XVI

How Scaramouch, in great need of Money, chanced to find a Gold Chain

THE time approaching when the Company of Players of *Palermo* must go to spend the Winter in *Rome*, *Scaramouch*, who had laid out nearly all his money on wedding-dresses and feasting, found himself in great want.

At the height of his distress he fortunately found a purse in which was a Gold Chain of the value of a hundred louis.[1] The sight of this precious metal dispelled all his sorrow; nevertheless he found himself in a new predicament because he feared that, in attempting to convert the chain into money, it might find its owner, and further, he deemed rightly that it was inadvisable to confide such a secret to anyone.

The *Marquis d'Aqua Viva* who had lost this Chain, having made announcement that he would give twenty pistoles to whoever restored it to him, *Scaramouch* planned to obtain the reward without giving up the Chain.

For this purpose he went to a Gilder of copper whom he ordered to make of this metal a Chain similar to the one he had found. Next, he sought out a good Monk to whom he gave a gold link which he had detached from the Marquis' Gold Chain, saying to him: "Reverend Father, I know

[1] A *louis* was a gold coin of the value of twenty francs.

who has the Gold Chain belonging to the *Marquis d'Aqua Viva*, but the one who found it must have thirty pistoles and will not part with it for less, since he is a family man burdened with a great many children." The good Father pressed *Scaramouch* to reveal to him the possessor of the chain, saying that he could be quite certain that *Monsieur le Marquis* would not be particular about ten pistoles.

But *Scaramouch* refused to trust him and resolutely told the Father that if he did not give him the thirty pistoles within twenty-four hours, the Marquis would be in danger of losing his Chain, and for the rest he confided this secret to him under the seal of confession.

The Father seeing that he maintained this resolution told him to return the next day at the same hour. He did not fail to keep this appointment and in return for the thirty pistoles which the Father counted out to him, he delivered to him the Chain of gilded copper in the same purse in which he had found the gold one. On taking leave of the Father, *Scaramouch* gave him a thousand blessings and returned full of joy to his wife who was as much pleased at her spouse's adventure as the Marquis was chagrined when the Father carried to him the copper Chain in place of the gold one he had hoped to recover.

CHAPTER XVII

How Scaramouch journeyed with his wife Marinette from Palermo to Rome

HAVING found ready money by his trickery, *Scaramouch* departed with the rest of the Company to *Rome*, but the excessive daintiness of his wife *Marinette* soon proved to him that whosoever thinks, when married, to live the most contented of lives is not long in repenting of having engaged in it.

For, although he greatly loved his wife, he could only bear with impatience her little ways, as affected as they were ridiculous, up to such a point, that having every moment some differences with her regarding this subject, he was the butt of his companions; the Comedians' character being never to spare one another and to search eagerly for opportunities to mock at everyone.

Marinette made the Coach stop at every moment, sometimes because she felt unwell, sometimes to make water and sometimes to pluck a flower which she espied in the fields.

Scaramouch kept his temper although, as we have said, he raged inwardly. But it was much worse when they had arrived at the Hostelry. *Marinette* found nothing to her liking; the steam from the cooking upset her, the wine was too sour or too sweet, the bread was too new or too stale, the soup was not salt enough and, to be brief, nothing pleased her. Despite that *Scaramouch* had taken pains to obtain for her the best bed in the whole house, she did not leave off crying out the whole night long that the feather bed overheated her and that a crease in the sheet had broken one of her ribs.

She complained even, although it was no longer the season for fleas, that one of these insects had made her suffer martyrdom from its bites.

Tired of hearing her, *Scaramouch* struck fire and having lighted a candle took a musket, with which he made pretence of wishing to kill the flea of which she complained.

This extravagant resolution having frightened her, she gave him a little more peace for the remainder of the night.

Another evening, *Scaramouch*, perceiving that after having rubbed her hands with a certain pomatum, his wife had gone to bed with her gloves on, took his place beside her, all booted and spurred. *Marinette*, feeling these scratch her legs, gave a loud shriek as if she had been mortally injured. *Scaramouch*, knowing her humours, only laughed and told her that it was to hunt the fleas with, and surely he could very well wear his boots in bed since she wore her gloves.

After quarrelling for a good hour, *Marinette* pulled off her gloves to make *Scaramouch* take off his boots and, each having made peace with the other, they sealed the pact with several kisses, which seemed to them as pleasant as fine weather after a storm, or health after an illness.

CHAPTER XVIII

How Marinette made her first appearance on the Stage

THE Company of Players having arrived at *Rome*, *Scaramouch* proposed that *Marinette* should appear on the Stage with them. To this the greater part of the youthful actors agreed, but rather to be in the good graces of the wife than with the design of pleasing the husband.

On the day when *Marinette* was to play the part of a *Soubrette*, after having put on a costume suitable to this character, and in which she appeared altogether charming, she told her husband to put in her busk, which he did.

To begin to make a name in the first town in the world, *Scaramouch* surpassed himself in this comedy and *Marinette*, pretty and well formed, being seconded by him, played so charmingly that she attracted the eager glances of the spectators.

The play being ended, a great number of *Nobles* came behind the Scenes to congratulate *Scaramouch*.

The incense which some of these *Gentlemen* burnt in honour of *Marinette's* beauty and charm was so strong, that she fell, half swooning, into an Armchair. The better to conceal her game, she began to inveigh against her husband and to burst into tears as if he had ill-treated her.

All these Noblemen strongly blamed *Scaramouch* and wished to learn the reason for her grief, but they were not a little surprised when she told them that her husband had put in her busk so cold that she was like to die of colic. They were gallant enough to find that she had cause for complaint and did not fail to tell *Scaramouch* to warm his wife's busk so well when he put it in the next time that she would never be obliged to ask this service of some other who perhaps would please her better.

CHAPTER XIX

How Scaramouch, having supped with the Duc de Carbognan, carried off a large pasty which broke upon his head

IN a very little while *Scaramouch* and *Marinette* saw themselves Owners of the Company which, owing to their renown, became the richest in all *Italy*. The *Roman* Nobles were not content to see them on the Stage only. Some went to visit *Marinette* to converse with her and hear her sing, others invited her husband to their houses in order to see his grimaces and postures at close quarters.

He never left these princely tables without taking home with him I do not know how many Fish-soups and Stews. One day, having seized upon a large oval Pasty at the *Duc de Carbognan's* and being unwilling to confide it to anyone, so much did he fear that so fine a dish might escape him, he carried it in his arms up to the door of his house; when, having placed it on his head to search in his pocket for the key, the bottom crust broke in such a manner that the Pasty descended on his shoulders like a *Spanish* ruff.

Having heard his voice, the Servant ran quickly to open the door, and seeing him in this state, believed at first that he had disguised himself expressly and that the Pasty was made of cardboard only; but when *Scaramouch* put his tongue out a foot long to lick up the sauce which ran down his face, he soon saw that it was not a counterfeit but truly made of meat and crust.

When he had gone upstairs to his room the Pasty was cut from his neck almost in the same manner in which a Galley-Slave's collar is filed through when he is set free.

The grease which had set over his eyes prevented him from seeing, on his entering, seven or eight Noblemen who were then with his wife and had brought with them a magnificent collation. Although *Scaramouch* most unseasonably came to disturb them, they were delighted at having witnessed so diverting an adventure, and one of them, taking a napkin, himself wiped *Scaramouch* clean and gave him a glass of wine to put him in good humour.

Having swallowed the comforting Cordial, *Scaramouch* took his seat at Table with them and served himself with one of the halves of his Pasty, which he liked very much better than all the Dainties with which the table was furnished. He soon consoled himself for his misfortune when he noticed that he was left to eat his Pasty by himself and that none ventured to touch it, which perhaps would not have happened if he had brought it home whole and sound. He was much gratified at having followed, without thinking of it, the precept of that famous Glutton who blew his nose in the best Dishes in order to have the pleasure of eating them all to himself.

CHAPTER XX

How Marinette was delivered of a boy ; how Scaramouch prayed Cardinal Chigi to be the God-father ; and how he obliged his Eminence to make him a present

HAVING visited during the Summer the principal towns of *Lombardy*, *Scaramouch* returned the following Winter to play at Rome. His wife had nearly reached her time to be brought to bed ot her first child when he arrived there: for which reason he did not leave her for a moment, and by amusing her, sought to allay the pain she suffered.

When she was in the agony of her labour, she did not cease screaming that *Scaramouch* was a trickster and had betrayed her. " Is this," she said, " how you promised never to make me big, you traitor, you impostor ? " " Do be quiet, do be quiet, my darling," replied *Scaramouch*, " forgive me for this once and I promise you that henceforth I myself will be brought to bed for you." " Is this then how you pretend to cherish me," added *Marinette*, " as if I did not know that such a thing were impossible ? " " Not at all, my dear," he replied, " there is a very creditable writer who says that Hares are male for one year and female for another, may not a man be the same ? "

Marinette being at last happily delivered of a

little *Scaramouch*, her husband went immediately to beg Cardinal *Chigi* to honour him by standing Godfather.

The Cardinal, who liked *Scaramouch*, willingly accorded him this favour and even went in person to the Church where the little *Scaramouch* was christened with great solemnity.

At the conclusion of the ceremony, his Eminence withdrew without making any present either to the Father, or to the Mother or even to his Godchild, contrary to the usual custom observed regularly in *Italy*.

A fortnight later, the Comedians having gone to play before the Queen of *Sweden*, *Scaramouch* cried out in the hearing of the Cardinal who was present there "*Miracolo, miracolo, Eminentissimo Signore.*[1] Your Godchild has begun to talk."

Impatient to learn what *Scaramouch* was hinting at, the Queen of *Sweden* asked him what his son could have said. "Madam," replied *Scaramouch*, "the child is complaining that his Eminence did not give him anything at his Christening."

The Cardinal with a smile immediately drew off the Diamond Ring which he had on his finger and gave it to *Scaramouch*, saying, "Here is something to keep him quiet."

Scaramouch thanked him humbly and told

[1] "A miracle, a miracle, Most Eminent Signor."

him that he would not fail to send his Godson to him so that he himself could thank him for it and, besides, he did not know if the child would not have something else to say to him.

The entire company burst into laughter at the pleasant means which *Scaramouch* had employed to induce the Cardinal to make him a present. The Carnival over, *Scaramouch* left *Rome* to spend Lent at *Florence* where he had purchased a fine piece of land just without the gate styled the *Pozzio Imperiale* and caused this inscription to be placed on the house :

Fiori Fiorilli,
E gli fu flora il fato,[1]

making allusion to his name *Fiorilli* and wishing to inform passers-by through these words that destiny had bestowed a happy abundance on his family.

CHAPTER XXI

How Scaramouch went to Milan

AFTER having remained at *Florence* for a length of time sufficient to put in good order the land he had acquired, *Scaramouch* passed into the Duchy of *Milan*, where his reputation was already so noised abroad that the

[1] Fate has caused the flowers of Fiorilli to bloom here.

Governor made him a present of a gold Chain as soon as he arrived.

On the stage, *Scaramouch* did not disappoint the good opinion that had been conceived of him ; and the scenes which he played in private were hardly less demonstrative of his natural gift of being a Comedian in all his actions.

One day, he went to the *Marquis de Caracene's* house, wearing the gold Chain to the end of which he had attached a paper bearing this Governor's image, who, at first, was annoyed by this ; but *Scaramouch* having told him that he had no other design than to inform everybody who had given him the Chain, the Marquis presented him with a fine gold Medallion stamped with his Portrait.

While he gained admiration at *Milan*, he and his Company were asked to *Vienna* to play at the Emperor's court. From another quarter Cardinal *Mazarin* begged Prince *Alexander Farnese* to persuade him to visit *France*.

Scaramouch, who had learned from hearsay of the greatness and generosity of *Louis XIV.*, did not hesitate a moment to refuse the Emperor's offer and, with the Prince of *Parma's* sanction, decided for *France*, where he arrived about the year one thousand, six hundred and sixty.

CHAPTER XXII

How Scaramouch went to France and of his Adventures on the Way

ON the road to *France*, *Scaramouch* had no light troubles from *Novaleze* to *Grande Croix*, for *Marinette* would not ride on the Mules which usually made this journey, asserting that she could not sufficiently separate her legs to bestride such great beasts. There remained nothing else but to go in a Sedan Chair carried by two men, to which she agreed on condition that *Scaramouch* would follow behind. As these Chairmen took a route where Mules cannot pass he was obliged to follow on foot like a Spaniel.

At a league and a half from where they had started, one of the Chairmen fell down and put his leg out of joint and, being unable to proceed, *Scaramouch* was forced to take his place and carry *Marinette* as far as *Grande Croix*, where he discovered some other Chairmen.

When they had traversed the Plain, as there was still enough Snow on the ground, *Scaramouch* put *Marinette* in a Sledge for fun, but no sooner was she seated than the driver, who had the word, went off like an arrow from a bow. You should have heard *Marinette* scream all the way from the moment the Sledge began to slide until it reached Laneberg where it stopped.

Scaramouch, who arrived there first, had all

the trouble in the world to pacify *Marinette* who wanted to scratch his face. After letting her vent her anger in bitter words, he mounted a horse, put her on the crupper behind him and in the evening arrived at a village Inn where there was only one bed, already occupied by two Merchants who were going to *Turin*.

CHAPTER XXIII

How Scaramouch got the Merchants out of their Bed

MARINETTE, tired out from her ride and learning that, to complete her discomfort, she must sleep on straw, began to curse the moment she had left *Italy*.

To quieten her, *Scaramouch* said that he had thought of a means to secure the Merchants' bed if only she would help him to play his part.

Marinette having replied that there was nothing she would not do to gain a bed, he begged the Host to light a fire in the room where the Merchants were asleep, since he had no other, and he and his wife would pass the night there on Chairs.

Having sat by the fire with *Marinette*, *Scaramouch* drew from his pocket a rope which he had taken off his valise and asked his wife for some

Soap, saying: "To-morrow, you know, I must hang a Highway Robber and I want the rope to be well greased because, although I am a Hangman, I must do my business properly: now my brother is a miserly wretch and to save two sols never uses soap and makes his poor patients languish.

"I am an honest man and I do my job with humanity, my Father has taught me all the most cunning tricks in our business and, thank Heaven, I have known how to profit by them, being able to flatter myself, without conceit, that I am the most skilful Hangman for a hundred leagues round.

"You saw the other day how I polished off those unfortunate wretches who had murdered a Postboy. Well, wife, could anyone have done it more deftly than I did? As their relatives had given me four pistoles I was quick finishing them off, although the Judge had ordered them to die on the wheel."

The Merchants who were not asleep, thought from this conversation that they really were the Hangman and his wife, and quietly slipping between the bedside and the wall, they left the room to complain to their Host for having put a Hangman with them.

As soon as *Scaramouch* saw them outside, he locked the door behind them and having turned the Sheets went to bed with his wife.

On the morrow he disclosed the trick to his Host, who laughed wholeheartedly. He pursued his journey and arrived at *Chambéry*, the capital of *Savoy*, where *Italian* is not understood.

Desiring to collect his Valise which was at the Custom House, he asked the Clerk for it in this manner, " *Monsieur le Maître Bourreau*,[1] give me my things " (he wished to say *Maître du Bureau*[1]). The Clerk, offended by this expression, gave *Scaramouch* a fine blow with his fist, who, on his side, did not remain with arms folded ; but they were quickly separated and those who had interposed themselves to make peace, laughed to their hearts' content at the droll misunderstanding which had so offended the Clerk.

Arrived at *Lyons*, *Scaramouch* went to lodge at *The Three Kings* and according to the *Spanish* proverb (*No ay ni Puta ny Ladron sin ninguna devotion*),[2] as it was a Wednesday, *Scaramouch* who like *Marinette* was fasting, asked for *Poison*[3] instead of *Poisson*[3] for his supper. The Servant of the house, believing that they were talking nonsense, went to tell her Mistress that these Foreigners were mad.

The Hostess herself went up to their room to

[1] *Bourreau*, hangman; *Bureau*, office. Two words of similar sound but widely different meaning.

[2] There is neither Whore nor Thief but owns to some religion.

[3] *Poison*, poison ; *Poisson*, fish. Two words of nearly similar sound, but widely different meaning.

learn what they required. *Scaramouch*, thinking to explain himself better, said to her : " Madam, be so good as to give us a *Brioche* "[1]; he meant to say *Brochet*,[1] but the Hostess, believing that their piety allowed them to eat only a *Brioche* for a meal, served with one.

Scaramouch and *Marinette* who had dined none too well that day, kept expecting to see the *Brioche* followed by something else, but seeing that nobody made it their business to serve them with anything further, *Scaramouch* went below to the Kitchen where he would have stormed all night in vain if some Merchants who understood *Italian* had not come to his aid.

Having understood that *Scaramouch* wished for Fish, they told him that it would take too long to prepare, but they had only to join them at their Table ; *Scaramouch* and *Marinette* willingly broke their fast to eat meat with the Merchants, whom they found so friendly that they resolved to engage places in the Stage-coach in order to go to *Paris* in their company.

[1] *Brioche*, a fancy bread; *Brochet*, a species of fish called pike. Two words of almost similar sound, but widely different meaning.

CHAPTER XXIV

How Scaramouch, accompanied by his Dog and his Parrot, appeared before the King

ARRIVED at *Paris*, *Scaramouch* considered for some while in what manner he would present himself to the King for the first time. Finally he decided to go in his *Scaramouch's* costume, over which he put his cloak.

As soon as he was ushered into His Majesty's presence he threw his mantle to the ground and was seen with his Guitar, his Dog and his Parrot. He made the most agreeable display with these two Animals which he had trained to perform their parts, so that one stood on the handle of the Guitar and the other on a low Stool, when he sang these words :

Fa la ut a mi modo nel cantar
Re mi si on non aver lingua a quel la
Che sol fa profession di farme star
Mi re resto in questo
La berinto ch' ogni mal discerno
Che la mi sol fa star in questo inferno

La mi fa sospirare la notte é il di
Re mi rar la non vol el Mi-o dolor
La fa far ogni canto sol per mi
Mi mi sol moro ristoro
Non son mai per aver in sin ch' io spiro
Che la sol fa la-mor, io Mi-ro mi-ro

These three animals played their parts so well that the King took a fancy to the middle one, which was *Scaramouch*, in such wise that from that time onward he had the honour to entertain this great Prince during more than thirty years, appearing always different in his style although he never changed his character.

He soon had the satisfaction of seeing himself engraved and even sculptured in marble. Cabinets and mantelpieces were decorated with his Bust and his image: in short, the Court and Town could not bear him out of their sight.

CHAPTER XXV

How Scaramouch displayed his wit to the King

ONE day, the King being at dinner and perceiving *Scaramouch*, was so gracious as to fill with his own hand a glass of foreign wine for him to drink, to see if he were a connoisseur. *Scaramouch* soon swallowed the wine and when the King asked him what country he thought it came from, he answered that the pleasure of drinking it had prevented him from giving his attention to the matter.

The King filled him a second glass saying, "You must think this time because you will have no more." At the second essay, *Scaramouch* divined that it was wine from *Piedmont*.

Cardinal *Mazarin* having taken him aside said to him: " *Scaramouch*, you can boast that the greatest Monarch in the world has filled you a glass of wine." Those about the Cardinal being seized with laughter at the reply which *Scaramouch* made to him, the King desired to know what this was, but none having dared to tell him, *Scaramouch* spoke to His Majesty and said that his Eminence having told him that he could boast that the most powerful Monarch in the world had filled his glass with wine, he had replied that he would not fail to tell this to his Baker.

The King, understanding from this discourse, that the honour he had paid *Scaramouch* did not provide him with bread, replied at once with an unparalleled generosity: " You will tell him also that I raise your pension by a hundred pistoles." *Scaramouch* thanked His Majesty and withdrew well content.

CHAPTER XXVI

How Scaramouch again displayed his wit to the King

TO play an *Italian* Comedy, the company must be composed of—

Two lovers
Three women, two for the serious and one for the comic parts
A Scaramouch, *Neapolitan*
A Pantaloon, *Venetian*
A Doctor, *Bolognese*
A Mezzetin and a Harlequin, both *Lombards.*

That is the reason His Majesty allows this Company an annual pension of fifteen thousand livres so that each Player has at least five hundred crowns.

The Troupe was complete when the Pantaloon fired a Pistol at the aged Octave with whom he had quarrelled.

Although he missed his enemy, this did not prevent his taking flight and returning to *Italy*, where he became a Priest.

The Company continuing to be without a Pantaloon, the King ordered *Scaramouch* to send for another and gave him fifty pistoles for the travelling expenses. *Scaramouch* took the money, it is true, but he scarcely troubled himself to execute His Majesty's Commands.

Five or six months later, the King, seeing that the Pantaloon did not appear to be forthcoming, remarked one day at Table : " I gave *Scaramouch* fifty pistoles to obtain a Pantaloon from *Italy*, but I greatly fear that he has squandered the money and hence the Pantaloon will not come."

Scaramouch immediately made his way through the press and feigning to have some secret to impart to the King and to wish to speak in his ear, said very loudly : " It is true Sire, that *Scaramouch* has squandered the fifty pistoles, but I beseech Your Majesty to tell nothing of this to the King."

The King began to laugh and commanded *Scaramouch* to be given another hundred pistoles ; fifty for himself and the other fifty for the Pantaloon, so that he could offer no more excuses.

The Queen, who had taken pleasure in *Scaramouch's* artlessness, asked him if his wife were with child and when she would be brought to bed. " That will be," he answered, " when it pleases Your Majesty ; my wife always makes it her duty to obey faithfully all Your Orders."

CHAPTER XXVII

How Scaramouch obliged the Queen Mother to present him with a winter suit

SCARAMOUCH having come to Court dressed, despite the intense cold, in a Coat and Breeches of Taffeta, was the laughing stock of the Courtiers; who rallying him said that apparently he had mistaken January for July; but to gain his end he patiently supported their jests, and pretending to be colder even than he really was, chattered his teeth and gave way to tears.

The Queen Mother, who was always moved by the sight of tears, wished to know for what reason he had to bewail thus. He replied: "Three misfortunes, Madam, have happened to me this morning.

"My faithful spaniel, which I loved as fondly as my wife, is dead. My Lackey has stolen all my clothes and left me only what I have on and lastly, to crown my misfortunes, as I was running, distracted, into my chamber, my Parrot began to scream: 'Thief! Thief!' I dealt it a cuff to punish it for crying out so tardily but wishing only to chastise it, I have killed it instead. While breathing its last it called me 'Traitor' a hundred times, and seeing itself near the grave, it sang so melodiously *Ut*, *Re*,

Mi, *Fa*, *Sol*, *La* that I am quite inconsolable for its Death.

" Behold, Madam, three mortal blows for poor *Scaramouch*, and I am so unfortunate as to be married, for were it not so, in my distress, I should go and shut myself up in a Monastery for the rest of my days ; already I play the Monk well enough, and besides it will be a fine opportunity to free myself from the importunity of my creditors, who do not cease to persecute me."

Touched by his plaints the Queen Mother ordered sixty louis to be given him with which to buy a Dog and a Parrot, and further permitted him to order a suit from the Court Tailor, the Court being then in mourning for the death of a foreign Prince.

Scaramouch, who had previously cried on account of the cold, now began to shed tears of joy, and having thanked the Queen Mother, he told her that her liberality had put him in a position to have clothes again, since he had a servant whose glib chatter would serve him in place of the Parrot ; but he despaired of ever being able to find a Dog like the dead one.

When the new clothes were ready, *Scaramouch* did not fail to wait upon the Queen Mother, who, seeing him tricked out in black with a long cloak of *Spanish* cloth lined with scarlet, did not know what to make of this extraordinary mixture and asked him why he was dressed so ; he replied that it was to conform to the Court which was then in mourning. " But," answered the Queen Mother, " there is no need to line your suit with scarlet." " That is," your Majesty, " because I wished to kill two birds with one stone, to wear mourning at once for my Parrot and for Prince N——"

His imagination was considered so fantastic and so droll, that it served to amuse the Court for above a fortnight.

CHAPTER XXVIII

Of Scaramouch's Person and Qualities

AS to *Scaramouch's* physical constitution he was, as I have said already, short-sighted, deaf in the left ear, and had one shoulder entirely withered. He was tall and very upright and remained so until extreme old age, and even then stooped but little. One thing worthy of remark is that although he was such a large eater, he was one of the most agile Players ever seen. He was very fond of women, with whom he had no great cause to be content, for the moods and caprices of his first wife plagued him to death and the ill-concealed intrigues of the second grieved him in the highest degree. In character, he was extremely suspicious, miserly and hot-tempered. He had a lively imagination but rarely spoke, having great difficulty in expressing in words what he wished to say but, in return, nature had endowed him with a wonderful talent which enabled him to explain by the postures of his body and the grimaces of his face, all that he desired ; and that in so original a manner that the celebrated Molière, who studied him for a long while, confessed frankly that he owed to him all the beauty of his gestures.

CHAPTER XXIX

How Scaramouch returned to Italy

IT is generally stated that those who make money do not know how to keep it. Thus *Scaramouch*, governed by the inconstancy so natural to Mankind, or by home-sickness, announced his intention of returning to *Italy* where his wife had remained for some years.

He asked leave of the Court which was granted him, on condition that he would return. This he promised, although in his heart he had resolved to stay there for good.

Before his departure he went to bid farewell to the principal Nobles at the Court, from each of whom he begged a pair of Riding-Boots for his journey. He received so many that he resold enough to fit out a Regiment of Cavalry. The money he obtained was more than sufficient to take him to *Florence*, where he purchased some more property. First, he had the great joy of seeing his wife again after such a long separation; but he had hardly stayed with her a fortnight when he wished he were far away.

Her fantastic moods had never left her and as *Scaramouch* was not so patient as of old, not a day passed but what they had high words.

Moreover, having relished the pleasant and polished manners of the *French*, he could not support those of the *Italians* which he found coarser. If he wished to live in the Country his servants enraged him, and the Peasants, knowing him to be extremely miserly, took a delight in robbing him of everything that passed through their hands.

This was the reason why *Scaramouch* eagerly sought for an opportunity to return to France, where he made himself admired and saw himself esteemed and loved more even than before.

CHAPTER XXX

How Scaramouch became enamoured of a Baker's Daughter in Paris

SCARAMOUCH had either brought back from *Italy*, like a sickness, the fantastic humour common enough to the people of that

Nation, or else because he was advancing in years, he had taken to the habits of old age ; for every day he gave his comrades some cause for discontent and quarrelled with them unceasingly and for the most part without any reason.

The amour which *Scaramouch* had on his mind came happily to procure them peace, because being engaged in this new passion, he thought only of winning the beauty's heart.

She was a Baker's daughter who for a work-girl was pretty enough and not more than fifteen or sixteen years old. Despite her youth she nevertheless was possessed of sufficient charms to attract *Scaramouch* for a long time, who at last after many entreaties, made her promise that he might come and see her one day when her father had gone to the country.

Although the girl had given her word, as her heart was very far from having the least inclination for him, she advised her father of her elderly lover's project and of the tryst she had given him.

The father who knew *Scaramouch* and who was delighted at being able to amuse himself at his expense, arranged with the girl that she would welcome him while he, pretending to have been unable to go to the country, would suddenly come and knock at the door so that she could force *Scaramouch* to conceal himself in a

Kneading-Trough, which she would close and lock so that he would be a prisoner inside.

All unconscious of the trick to be played upon him, *Scaramouch* betook himself at the appointed hour to his Mistress's house, with all the hope that an amorous old man is capable of conceiving.

But hardly had he begun to show by his compliments how fortunate he esteemed himself at having a private interview, when the Father suddenly knocked on the door.

The daughter feigned astonishment, " Ah ! " said she, " I am undone, my father will kill you if he finds you here."

Scaramouch who trembled in good earnest, asked her if there were no place where he could hide. The girl at once showed him the Trough where he crouched among the remains of the flour. She then opened the door to her father who was knocking louder and louder.

Having come in, the father did not omit to grumble at his daughter and to tell her that he wanted his supper ; and that he had not gone to the country on account of the bad weather.

The girl obeyed and prepared the supper for her father who went to bed in the same room where the Trough was, in which *Scaramouch* passed the whole night very ill at ease, because he did not dare to breathe or complain for fear of being found out.

The next day, as he hoped, his Mistress would

come and set him free and make him forget all his sufferings in the favours she would infallibly accord him.

A crony of the Baker's who was in the secret, came to him to suggest buying the Trough, to which proposal the Baker willingly agreed. The visitor having concluded the bargain, had the Trough taken down into the street by some men well posted. *Scaramouch's* fright can be imagined, who did not know where he was to be taken.

When the Trough was in the street, it was opened and *Scaramouch*, recovering all his former vigour, jumped out so quickly that the bystanders who were waiting to ridicule him were themselves surprised. *Scaramouch*, white all over from the flour, ran as if he had a fire at his buttocks and wherever he went made all the children flock together, who pursued him shouting " Guy ! Guy ! "

CHAPTER XXXI

How Scaramouch became enamoured once more, and of his second Marriage

NOTWITHSTANDING *Scaramouch's* ill-luck in his amour with the Baker's daughter, it did not prevent him from pledging his heart anew to another Work-Girl, still more beautiful than the first and not so unassailable.

The necessitous state to which she was reduced made her listen with sincere intentions to the old man ; and through the intrigue of a certain Old Clothes Woman, she gave herself wholly to *Scaramouch* who lodged her in his house. She lived there for many years in pleasant enough harmony, but at last, following that inclination inseparable from her sex, she left him for a young spark who took her to *England* whence she returned a year later.

Scaramouch, who loved her tenderly, took her back, and though she still bore unmistakable signs of her unfaithfulness, he loved her just as much as ever insomuch that having learned that his wife *Marinette* had died in *Italy*, he married her.

He could not afford her greater proofs of his affection : but the new wife, however, unmindful of so much kindness and seeing herself united to him by an inseparable bond, gave him daily just cause for complaint and regret at having made her fortune.

Scaramouch who did not ignore the fact that it is difficult for a young wife with a husband of eighty years to keep virtuous, pretended to be even more short-sighted than he really was, and to overlook many things which he saw only too well.

But observing at last that she scorned disguise and maintained neither reserve nor prudence, he had her put in Prison, and thence transferred to a Convent, where she soon died of sorrow and despair.

CHAPTER XXXII

Of Scaramouch's Covetousness

AS I have said already *Scaramouch* was naturally avaricious and old age had increased this passion in him, so much so that for fear the servant might make a market penny, he himself went to market to buy two deniers'[1] worth of herbs as well as all the other provisions needed for the house, and although he was known by everyone, great and small, he never troubled to hide his purchases, but returned from market holding his handkerchief in his hand as men do in *Italy*.

As he always insisted on a good bargain he was shown only the worst of everything, whether it was meat or fish, and so long as it was a ridiculous price, he bought all without troubling whether the meat was putrid or the fish stank,

[1] *Denier*, money of account equal to one-twelfth of a *sol* or *sou*.

because he had so poor a nose that he smelt nothing.

He enjoined two things above all from his servants ; never to tell him what his wife did or how the meat smelt, not wishing that his imagination should be offended by unpleasant thoughts which his weak senses did not permit him to discover.

Thus *Scaramouch* possessed the secret of furnishing his table at little cost, but he never invited anyone, and he took great care to have it said that he was not within to those who desired to speak with him during his dinner hour, for fear that it would cost him a glass of wine.

When he was invited out he ate largely of whatever was newest in season, such as Peas, Asparagus, and Mushrooms ; but he never ate them at home until they were almost out of season, stating for his reason that it was not good for the health ; thus he could always find something amiss with anything that was expensive.

CHAPTER XXXIII

How Scaramouch made a comical Mistake in regard to his Servant

ONE day a little girl whom *Scaramouch* had brought up in his house like a child of his own, begged the servant to let her sleep in the kitchen, telling her that her bed was better than the one in which she slept; but in truth because she had a mind to talk during the night with a youthful neighbour whose window opened directly opposite the kitchen.

The servant, suspecting nothing, willingly fell in with her wishes, and having given up her bed, went to sleep in the little girl's, which was in the room next to that of *Scaramouch*.

The good man who, owing to a Love-Letter having fallen into his hands, had discovered the little girl's amour, rose very early to whip her in bed, where he found the servant whom he lashed with the utmost vigour, taking her to be the little girl; the Servant cried out in vain that he was making a mistake, but *Scaramouch* who was almost deaf and blind did not leave her until his anger was completely appeased.

Perceiving that *Scaramouch* still thought that he had whipped the little girl, the servant did not dare to undeceive him for fear of being grumbled at after having had the thrashing.

CHAPTER XXXIV

Another example of Scaramouch's Covetousness

IT must be remarked that *Scaramouch* lived eighty-seven years without ever having had any other illness but that which put him in his grave, if the extinction of natural heat can be called an illness: because he died without an attack of fever.

His Physician having advised him to take a cooling Remedy, he summoned an Apothecary with whom he bargained for over an hour; but the Apothecary having told him that he could not make it for less than thirty sols on account of the cost of the drugs it must contain, he resolved, not without much ado, to command it on that understanding.

The Apothecary having returned with the remedy, *Scaramouch* again disputed with him for above ten minutes in endeavour to beat down the price; but the Apothecary giving him to understand that the remedy would lose all its virtue if it became cold, he placed himself in a position proper to receive it, which made the Apothecary roar with laughter.

Hardly had he received half of it when the thought of the thirty sols, which the Operation was to cost him, made him tell the Apothecary to stop, who, thinking that the medicine was too hot, ceased immediately: then *Scaramouch* put on his spectacles and made him open the syringe to see how much remained, and finding that he had only taken exactly half, pulled out fifteen sols from his pocket which he gave to the Apothecary, telling him that he could sell the rest to someone else; since for his part he had enough of it.

CHAPTER XXXV

How Scaramouch, during his sickness, made a present to his Servant

SCARAMOUCH having called his servant, began to regale her with a long sermon on fidelity: " You are well aware, *Margot*," he said to her, " that in this life there is nothing dearer to us than the salvation of our souls; hence I counsel you to return, before I die, anything that you may have taken from me.

" For my part, I shall satisfy my conscience by leaving you something to reward you for the time you have served me, and particularly so that you may remember me."

Margot protested that she had nothing to restore to him, and thanked him for his kind intentions towards her; and believing that he would give her something of great value, she went down on her two knees and asked his blessing.

Scaramouch touched to see her in such modest countenance, and regarding her with a pitiful eye, said: " Listen, *Margot*, I wish to add another gift to the one I had thought of making you ; for besides a receipt for making herb tea, I give you further this Memorandum of money which was owed me and has now been paid.

" But alas ! you are too faithful, I must give you something more ; go at once and take a red box from my chest and bring it to me."

The servant hastened to look for the box, which she found at the bottom of the chest after taking out all the contents. She gave it to *Scaramouch* who opened it and withdrew a truss which he gave to her, saying: " I must be very fond of you, my dear *Margot*, to present you with this beautiful truss which is quite new ; but I do not regret it in the least and I pray God to give you grace to make use of it ; go, you have well deserved it, I give it to you with all my heart: but above all take care never to boast of my generosity, it is enough that you have proof of it."

Margot was so put out at such a discourse, that she could not refrain from telling him what she thought of him, but the good man heard nothing, or else he would not have failed to style her ungrateful and thankless.

CHAPTER XXXVI

How Scaramouch made a present to his Lackey

SCARAMOUCH had a Lackey who had served him for a considerable time, for the sole reward of seeing him perform his postures and being able to go to the Playhouse without paying.

Having affectionately embraced him and recommended him always to walk in the fear of God, *Scaramouch* said to him : " My dear *Brindavoine* (because he was called so) I know you are a good fellow, and I know that you have served me with all your zeal, for nearly seven years without wages ; I wish now to repay you with interest, so that you will pray to God for me with all your heart in the event of my dying soon ; but if I can credit an Astrologer who told me that I should attain the age of one hundred and twenty years, you are like to grow old in my service without its costing you a single double,[1] and I can promise you that I shall never speak to you of wages, because that displeases you ; but at least permit me now to take the liberty of giving you something for the excellent and agreeable services you have rendered me."

Brindavoine answered that *Scaramouch* was his master and that he had never doubted his affection. *Scaramouch* embracing him again,

[1] *Double,* a coin worth the double of a *denier,* or one-fifth of a *sol.*

said to him: "Here now is a little sack which I give you, wherein you will find all my Masterpieces. My greatest regret is not being able to leave you also the postures and grimaces with which I season them, those I used when I wished to make people laugh, or those I employed when I desired to frighten them.

"Since I cannot bequeath you so precious a gift, I wish to make your fortune in another manner, by giving you my *Scaramouch's* costume which is still quite new, for I have not worn it for nearly five years, and it is of so fine a cloth that even after all the somersaults I have made during more than twenty years, it does not show the slightest tear.

"You can hire it out during Carnival, and provided you say it was mine, everyone will want to go as *Scaramouch*—although the name does not make the Player. If the Old-Clothes Dealers gain so much from hiring out Disguises, their profits will be as nothing compared with yours; moreover, it will serve you for a suit of mourning in case I should die.

"This is, my dear *Brindavoine*, the greatest mark of friendship a Master can show to a faithful servant, and if I may speak so, of a father for his child; because if I had a second son, I should not leave him any other heritage."

CHAPTER XXXVII

How Scaramouch made a present to his Surgeon

A YOUNG Surgeon who had formerly tended *Scaramouch* for a wound in the head, caused by his falling from the top to the bottom of a staircase, came to visit him some days before his death, and seeing beyond all question, that he had not long to live, said to him: " At last, Signor *Tiberio*, you must think of death and put your conscience in order."

" That I have done already," retorted *Scaramouch*, " it is only two days ago since I received the Sacrament ; nevertheless, I do not think to die soon, and a sign that I shall still live a long time is," he added, showing his swollen legs, " that I am becoming stouter."

He was then in an Armchair, where he was forced to remain during the last days of his illness for fear of being suffocated if he were put to bed. After having spoken of one thing and another, *Scaramouch* said: " I remember that I have never given you anything, except a free ticket for the Comedy, in return for your having cured me of a wound in the head, it is only just to recognise so excellent a service."

He said these words in so serious a tone, that the Surgeon thought that he was going to give him a sum of money.

But *Scaramouch* taking from his pocket an old

pair of spectacles, with some waste paper, said: " Here, Sir, take these Spectacles which have served me nearly sixty years, they can in good truth be termed immortal, besides they have fallen off a thousand times without being broken.

" As you may grow older and need them to let blood, I make you a present of them, as well as of my Songs, which it is true are not set to music, but you are a man of parts, you will not fail to devise Airs on those I used."

The Surgeon so far from being angry, could not restrain from laughing at this conversation, and taking his leave said that *Scaramouch* wished to play a Comedy until the day of his death.

CHAPTER XXXVIII

How Scaramouch made a present to his Physician

SCARAMOUCH having sent for his *Physician*, said to him: " My dear friend, I perceive clearly that it is time for me to go and discover what is happening in the other World, since I have been so long in this one.

" You have always thought me very mean, because I have never invited you to come and sup with me, for all the twenty years we have known each other ; I swear to you that this has never been due to any covetousness, but simply because I have heard it said that Physicians no more forgive their friends than their enemies. Therefore before I die, I wish to show you a mark of my generosity.

"I had two excellent Guitars ; one of them I gave to a friend of my late wife's, who played it so beautifully that he often made her swoon with delight.

"The other one I have saved for you ; it is one of old *Vauban's*, there is no need to say more : in addition to its soothing my sorrows and headaches, it possessed moreover the virtue of charming away the pain caused by my piles.

"I advise you to employ it in the same manner and to play Minuets, Corantos, and Chaconnes, to your patients ; instead of prescribing them Purges, Clysters and Lettings of Blood. If it does not cure them, at any rate it will never kill them. Farewell, dear friend, leave me, for it is easy for me to die without your aid."

CHAPTER XXXIX

How Scaramouch gave up the Ghost

SCARAMOUCH seeing that his appetite waned more and more began to think that he truly had not long to live : however he still ate every morning a soup with two pounds of bread, a large chicken, and drank his pint of Burgundy. In the evening he would take soup, eat a chicken, three biscuits, and drink another pint of the same wine.

He held to this manner of living for the space of three months, until he was troubled with a kind of dysentery due to a surfeit of melon.

The day before he died he ordered for his dinner an *Italian* soup, that is to say a great dish of *Vermicelli*, with *Parmesan* cheese.

His Physician who had come to see him again, told him that this would be harmful to his health and if he were careful he might live another week or more.

" Are you quite certain ? " asked *Scaramouch*. " Yes," replied the Physician. " Ah well ! a week more or less," he added, " is a trifle for a man who has lived so long, and is not worth the trouble of depriving myself of a fine dish of *Vermicelli ;* let me have plenty of soup and send for my Confessor."

After he had conferred some time with him to whom he had entrusted the care of his soul, he ate his dish of *Vermicelli* and drank more even than usual. In the evening he doubled the dose, and ate with as good an appetite as he had ever had.

But alas ! there came the fatal moment when death had resolved to cut short the course of so fine a life.

Two hours after midnight, seeing that he could not sleep, he called three young Journeyman Upholsterers who lived in the same lodging, with whom he played at cards. Some moments later he said to them : " Continue my children, amuse yourselves, but do not interrupt my prayers."

For a quarter of an hour he recited in a loud voice many Prayers which he knew by heart ; and when he came to those words of the Lord's Prayer *Sicut in coelo & in terra*,[1] he heaved a sigh which was the last in his life.

In addition to a considerable legacy which he left to a Religious Institution, he bequeathed to his son, who is a learned Priest of considerable merit, all the estate he possessed in *France* and *Italy*, which amounted to nearly one hundred thousand crowns.

Such was the end of the most illustrious Comedian who ever has appeared on an *Italian* Stage, and it can be said without exaggeration,

[1] In Earth as it is in Heaven.

that Nature after having made him had broken her mould.

He has been lamented by everyone, and even by his Comrades, although for five years he took his share from the Company without playing for it. An extraordinary concourse of all manner of persons followed his body to the Church of St. Eustace, where he was buried with great pomp on the eighth day of December, 1694.

LIST OF ILLUSTRATIONS

The Cover of this Book has been designed by
Randolph Schwabe The Typography
and Binding have been arranged
and the Book produced by
Cyril W. Beaumont

Printed by
C. W. BEAUMONT, 75 Charing Cross Road, London, W.C. 2.

www.ingramcontent.com/pod-product-compliance
Lightning Source LLC
Chambersburg PA
CBHW030414310726
48979CB00002B/409

* 9 7 8 1 9 0 6 8 3 0 4 0 3 *